LETHAL LEGACY:

Thrill Of The Hunt 2

A Novel By

Sir Patrick Bijou

DESCRIPTION

***

Detective Andrew Martin had been in the homicide division of the Baltimore police force for twelve of his seventeen years in law enforcement. For the most part he loved his job except for the kind of cases that he was currently working on.

There was a string of unsolved murders the last count was ten that was driving him nuts. The problem was that the deaths had several things in common, they were all young healthy males, all of them had been drained of blood, and each of them had had a set of puncture marks that looked as if they were made by large bore needles that were surrounded by bright red lipstick.

Through some basic profiling it was determined that the killer was indeed female although it was rare for a serial killer to be female, she was between the ages of twenty-five to thirty-five, Caucasian and that she would have a well above average intelligence.

WHO IS THIS VAMPIRE KILLER?

The Question seems unsolvable but things changed when Agent Amelia comes in to help.

But What Happens After?

ABOUT THE AUTHOR

***

Sir Patrick is an eclectic writer, lives in the United Kingdom and was born in 1958 in Georgetown and raised in London, England.

His diverse writing prowess has been influenced by many experiences.

He pursued several courses of study at several universities, and declared two majors during his schooling which included the areas of Business and Economics and finally obtained his doctorate in Economics and International banking.

In all these scholastic studies though, the true treasures he took away are not the certificates (though those are very important), but instead the experiences he had, the people he met, the foods he ate and even the places he stayed.

"In truth, I am a citizen of the world and this greatly influences my writing.

So, if you are already a fan of mine, I appreciate you. If you are not yet one, then what are you waiting for? Read a book and then read some more. I create characters that resonate with you and infuse life into all I write".

Finding my Books:

Sir Patrick has written over 15 published fictional and non-fictional books across several genres, I have realized the need to make it easier for my readers to find my books.

TABLE OF CONTENTS

CHAPTER 1

***

Andrew looked at the clock on the computer, realized they had been going at it for over sixty hours, and knew that they should take a break get cleaned up, eat something, and get a few hours' sleep then start back on it with fresh eyes. Amelia quickly agreed. Vampires could go long hours between rest periods with no physical effects but their mental facilities would start to dim and they knew they needed to be sharp or they could miss an important piece of information. The two of them headed into the kitchen to find some food and more importantly blood, it had been days since they drank any and they were both getting extremely hungry now that they had taken a break.

When Amelia and Andrew entered the kitchen, Susan took one look at them and frowned, "The two of you should know better. Why in the hell would you go so long without blood? Are you trying to go feral?" Susan admonished sternly.

"I will admit we are hungry but we are nowhere near starving. We just got busy and forgot to feed no big deal," Andrew replied shrugging his shoulders.

"Andrew both you and Amelia lips are thinned and pale that is a sure sign that you are not just hungry but starving when was the last time you took blood?" Susan asked her tone showed her displeasure.

"Umm! About four or five days ago but I have been eating food," Andrew replied defensively.

"Andrew you have to drink blood every two to three days and eat least twice a day by the way candy bars and chips don't count." Susan admonished sternly.

"Ok, we will start eating and taking blood regularly." Andrew promised.

Amelia handed Andrew a glass of blood and an egg sandwich. Just as the two of them started eating, Charles came walking into the kitchen. "We have an ID on the shooter/bomber, his name was Alex Maslin. He was a young werewolf whose parents were killed by vampire three years ago. According to the leader of the local were community he tried unsuccessfully to get other Weres to rise up against vampires. After numerous attempts he just disappeared until today." Charles interrupted before Susan could continue. He then handed a file containing the pertinent information on their suspect.

"Do you think Amsu was involved with his attack?" Amelia asked after she started to read over the file. She handed it over to Andrew. He quickly read the file one thing that stood out was the fact that Maslin lacked the ability to build a device like the one that was used. He also noted that there was no indication that he had the sophistication to plan such an attack. Andrew knew there was a backer who had planned and most likely financed the operation.

"No I believe he was involved how else Maslin would have gotten the information he needed to plan the attack. From what Sam had told me he was just a poor hurting confused kid who let his anger over ride his common sense. Sam has offered to help us in the investigation. He owns a large computer security company. Cindy his wife has also offered her services she is supposed to be one of the top computer security specialists in the country. She has helped the Feds with a couple of cases from what I understand," Charles explained.

"So, Sam is the local Alpha?" Andrew asked.

"Andrew you really have to let that story book stuff go. Weres do not live in compounds or caves the live-in houses and apartments. They do not have alpha's or such as leaders. Sam is the leader of local community because he was asked to be, mainly because his business has led to him having good contacts with humans and in a small part because of my friendship with him. He acts as a liaison between his people and us. He has been a good friend of mine for the last fifty years," Charles retorted shaking his head amused.

"Amelia, would you please try to find who Maslin associated with? I don't think he had the ability to plan and carryout an operation such as this alone. Charles or Susan do either of you have any contacts in the press I was wondering why they were at the mall." Andrew asked as he was trying to make sure he didn't forget anything.

"I have a friend he is an assignment editor for channel twenty-nine. I will give him a call and let you know what I can find out," Charles offered.

Amelia used the identity that Charles had given to her to log into the federal database looking to see what they had on the bombing and found that the information had been moved to a restricted database that Amelia couldn't find any files; it was as if the feds never investigated the incident. She had seen agents from both the FBI and the ATF there so she knew there had to be records. She tried to use every back door she knew of to find the information with no luck. Amelia picked up the phone and dialed a now familiar number.

What the fuck is going on here?" Amelia muttered as she waited for the phone to be answered

"What is a matter hun?" Andrew asked taking note of the apprehension in Amelia's voice.

"I can't seem to find any records of a federal investigation into the attack. I know I saw a half of dozen FBI and ATF agents there but there is no record of the event even happening according to the federal Government." Amelia mentally told Andrew while she quickly said, "Charles, we may have a problem here. I can't find any records on the attack in the FBI or DOJ databases."

"I will be right there, "Charles quickly responded before disconnecting the call.

Less than five minutes later Charles entered the room Flanked by Sam and Cindy. After Amelia gave them, a brief accounting of her activities Cindy quickly started using her aces to search the federal database trying to locate what information they had. Charles started making phone calls to his various contacts to try to figure out what was going. After several hours of work, they had managed to find out that someone had managed to make all of the information on the attack go away including the dozens of videos that had been posted on social sites. Whoever was behind the removal of the information was very meticulous as Amelia and the other could tell they hadn't missed a thing. Charles started calling his contacts in the federal government trying to ascertain where the information had gone. While Charles was working his contacts, Sam called an associate in the local Prosecutor's office. David Argils was an assistant DA. "Hey Sam what is up?" David cheerfully greeted his old friend recognizing the number from the caller ID.

"How's it hanging fleabag? I need a favor if you can do it." Sam replied.

"First of all I don't have fleas and what can I do for you? You know if I can help I will," David replied laughing.

"The bombing at the mall what can you tell me about the investigation. The victims were Charles' head of security and his wife." Sam asked.

"I have no idea what you are talking about. I have to go, but how about the two of us having a couple of drinks tonight at Sanguinem." David responded sounding cheerful but Sam could hear the underlying tension in his voice.

"Is eight good for you and why don't you bring Helen I know Cindy would love to see her." Sam suggested.

"I sure will it will be nice to get together." David said before ending the call.

Sam was concerned with David's reaction it was out of character for him to want to meet at Charles nightclub especially on a work night. Therefore, whatever was happening had David worried. Sam figured he would find out what David knew tonight. "Charles what are the chances of getting a VIP room at Sanguinem tonight? David asked.

"Very good in fact if you want you can use mine." Charles offered.

"Thank you. I think it may be a good idea if you, Andrew and Amelia were close-by he may want you to hear what he has to say," Sam suggested.

"We will be there. I would also like to bring Susan my mate with me," Charles replied.

"Congratulation about time you mated. I am looking forward to finally meeting her," Sam said offering his hand.

After Charles was done talking with Sam, Amelia asked if she and Andrew could talk to him in private for a few moments about a sensitive matter. Unsure what was going on Charles suggested they meet in Susan's private office because he knew that not only was it sound proof even from the most sensitive ears it was also constantly swept for bugs. Amelia and Andrew followed Charles down to the office and waited until he indicated it was all right for them to start the conversation.

"Charles, we have checked through all of the people that had knowledge of Catherine's and Emma's plans the day of the attack and have eliminated all but two suspects. We would like your permission to start an active investigation into them and to search their residents without them being aware of the searches," Andrew explained.

"Andrew, you and Amelia have been asked to find out where Amsu is and to dismantle his organization by any means necessary. You have my full confidence. May I ask who you suspect?" Charles replied a bit apprehensively.

"Kirk Morrow who was Mitch's assistant he was having serious money trouble until recently he managed to pay it off and deposited seventy- five grand into an off shore account. I cannot find a source for the money. The other is Christina Morehouse, Emma's office manager and in my mind, the more likely suspect. She has been receiving a monthly payment of twenty grand for the last two years from a shell company that Mark has determined is a subsidiary of a holding company owned by Layla. We did check her stock portfolio and couldn't find any records of buying stock in the company. I know it is possible it is just a coincidence but I have never been a strong believer in coincidences." Andrew replied making sure not to leave out anything that was important. He was so glad that he didn't have to go by human laws anymore it made thing a lot easier and quicker.

"Kirk got the money from me. He sold me a couple hundred acres of land he owned in Australia. I was trying to keep the sale off the radar so to speak so I could build a hideaway there. As far as his money trouble he invested too much into the housing bubble and lost his ass." Charles explained.

"OK, then I suppose we can remove him from the suspect list for now. I am still going to ask him about the calls he made to Egypt over the last few months if you have no objections." Andrew replied.

"That is fine but I suspect it is just that he is talking to his sister Kerrie." Charles stated with a shrug.

"Thank you. You just saved us a lot of time. What about Ms. Morehouse can you offer any insights into her?" Andrew asked glad that they could eliminate one of their suspects.

"I don't know her all that well. Amelia could just probe her thoughts and see if she can determine if they are the guilty party." Charles suggested off handedly.

"I can do that but I didn't want to do anything like that until I talked to you about it. Even if I try to do it subversively, there is a real chance that I would be caught. I am not sure how she would take it but I imagine she would be less than happy about it." Amelia responded.

"We had discussed the possibility of doing it but decided to wait until after we talked to you. The last thing we would want to do is cause dissention among your employees especially right now." Andrew explained finishing the explanation that Amelia had started.

Charles shook his head and chuckled. He had never heard of or seen two more in tuned mates in all his time it was as if they had a direct link to each other's thoughts.

He had watched them work and was surprised that they always seemed to know exactly what the other was thinking even when it was obvious that neither one of them was mentally talking to each other. Charles wasn't sure if he was jealous or thankful, he didn't share that deep of a connection with Susan.

"I would suggest you talk to Emma and if she can't offer you explanation; then either probe her mind or do a normal interrogation on her. I will support whatever you decide as will Susan." Charles promised.

Amelia and Andrew found Emma in the office she was sharing with her parents. Andrew knocked on the door announcing Amelia and his arrival. Emma looked up from her computer and smiled. "Hey guys how is the investigation going?" Emma cheerfully asked.

"Not too bad, that is why we are here. We could use your help." Andrew answered as he kissed her on the cheek

"What can I do for you this fine day?" Emma teased as she hugged Amelia.

"What can you tell us about your office manager Christina Morehouse? We spotted a couple of flags when we were running a back ground check on her." Amelia explained as she took a seat.

"She is very good at her job and is well respected by the people under her. She is very task oriented and dependable. Why were you running a back ground check on her what kind of flags did she trip?" Emma inquired suddenly very interested.

"We compiled a list of all the people who had known that you would be the one who was accompanying Catherine to her last doctor's appointment. Once we got the list together, we started trying to narrow down our list of potential suspects. We went through phone records and found out that only two of the people on the list mad regular calls to the Middle East; one was Kirk Morrow who was calling Cairo..." Amelia explained.

"Kirk is calling Kerri she is working for the Museum of Egypt Antiquities. She is an assistant curator." Emma explained interrupting Amelia.

"Your dad had explained that and the other concerns we had about Kirk. We are hoping you can do the same For Ms. Morehouse." Amelia continued.

"I can try but like I said I don't know her that well," Emma replied.

"Do you know of any reason why she would be receiving a monthly payment of twenty grand from one of Layla's holding companies?" Andrew asked.

"That is a good question one I would love to have the answer to." Emma responded in an even tightly controlled tone.

"Emma since she is your employee how would you rather, we handle this? We can either take a look at her residence without her knowledge, have Amelia attempt read her mind subversively or we can confront her with what we know and see if she can provide reasonable explanations why she is receiving the money." Amelia asked as she handed Emma the file with the information they had gathered on Ms. Morehouse.

"I would prefer you to interrogate her directly and if she doesn't cooperate fully then get your answers by any means necessary." Emma answered firmly after reading the file over. Then as an afterthought Emma added," You know she was one of the few people who had access to yours and Andrew's file."

Andrew's eyes darkened briefly. "Most interesting fact, I shall add that fact to our list of items we need to clear up with her," Andrew darkly stated.

"Andrew, we need proof of her betrayal. You must maintain control so we can find just how deep the rot goes." Amelia beseeched.

"No worried love, I am not losing control. I was just imagining what I would like to do to her if she did betray us," Andrew responded with a laugh.

The friends talked for a while planning on how they wanted to proceed. They decided to approach her just before she was supposed to leave for the evening and take her in to custody. Emma had arranged for a couple men from security to watch her discretely. Security also would be the ones to apprehend her and bring her to interrogation.

Christina Morehouse day was just about over it had been a trying day and to top it off she has had this foreboding feeling all day she almost didn't return form lunch but she knew if she did take off for no apparent reason she would be questioned. Since the latest attack, everyone in the office had been walking on eggshells not wanting to draw attention to themselves. There had been a rumor going around that someone on the inside had been helping Amsu and with the increased security, it was making it harder for her. She knew her time here was coming to an end and decided she wouldn't be returning after today. She looked up and saw it was time to go for the day she quickly shut off her computer and graved her bag to leave when Kirk Morrow and Dawn Avilla approached her. "I need you to come with us." Kirk ordered in a quiet tone.

Christina swallowed involuntarily and her shoulder slumped. "Kirk I really need to go I have a date tonight." Christina pleaded as she turned to walk away.

Dawn stepped in front of her and grabbed her by the arm. "It wasn't a request Christina. Either you can walk with us or I will handcuff you and drag you from here by your hair. Your choice," Dawn demanded in a low tone.

Christina's lowered her head bin defeat knowing she was caught her only hope that her death would be quick and merciful. She saw that they were drawing a crowd and tried to think how to use it to her advantage. "Why are you doing this to me? I already told them I wouldn't reveal any of their secrets once I leave what more does she want?" Christina begged with tears in her eyes.

Five of the other office workers stepped forward and stood blocking Kirk and Dawn's way. "Why are you treating her like this?" One of the larger males angrily asked.

Amelia and Andrew stepped out of Emma's office to see what the commotion was about and as soon as Christina saw them, she immediately Screamed," My god they are going to turn me over to her to wipe my mind like she did to Gregori Demidov."

The group of employees was getting antsy and started to crowd around to see what was going to happen to their friend. As far as they knew, she had been a good employee and was always friendly and helpful to all of them. There was more and more murmuring about how unfair it was to try to stop her from getting a better job. The mood was turning uglier by the second. A large vampire named Arnold Hatfield stepped forward from the rest of the group and approached Kirk and Dawn. "Why are you harassing Ms. Morehouse all she wants to do is improve her situation? I always thought Ms. Black was a fair woman." Arnold asked as he took a defensive stance.

Kirk knew Arnold was a Cossack who was turned in the middle of the fourteenth century. Unlike most of his kind Arnold served in every major war from the time, he was turned until Nam. After Nam, he decided to give war a break and study business management then accounting. Even though he was now a desk jockey as he called it, he was still a formable foe. Kirk knew he would have to tread carefully so as not to inflame the big man in front of him. "Arnold, you know dam well Ms. Black is more than fair. The Barnes are running security checks on everyone associated with the Black's companies and there are a couple of issues they need to discuss with her," Kirk explained patiently.

"What is she accused of?" Arnold asked suspiciously.

"I can't answer that Arnold but knowing Christina it is just a misunderstanding." Kirk stated hoping to defuse the situation.

Emma came out of her office and handed Amelia a piece of printer paper then approached the crowd of people who gathered watching the events. "I would think that I had earned more faith from you all than this. The Barnes are running back ground and security checks on everyone associated with my father including Neil and myself. Now as far as Christina I would like to know when she was going to tell me she leaving since I have never received word of her resignation. It makes me wonder what she is so afraid of." Emma announced. She then paused as she slowly looked around the room making eye contact with every one before settling her gaze on Christina. Everyone was watched as Christina bowed her head as Emma continued, "Well Christina would you like to explain why you are acting in this manner?"

Christina just started to walk towards the conference room where she assumed the interview was going to take place. She was well aware that everyone's eyes were on her. As she walked, she wondered how she would be executed, she had heard from the rumor mill that the last time someone had betrayed Charles, Susan had him encased in concrete then dropped into the Pacific. She walked into the room and Kirk told her to take a seat that Andrew would be with her in a couple minutes.

While Emma was addressing her employees, Amelia read the paper that Emma had handed her and wasn't overly surprised when she saw that the fax machine at Christina's desk had called the Holiday Express by the airport ten minutes before she was shot by Antonio Munoz. Andrew's eyes darkened with anger as he read over Amelia's shoulder, he slowly imagined Christina begging for mercy as he striped layer after layer of her skin. Amelia lightly rapped him across the back of the head to get him to focus on the real problem. They needed to find out how much information she had passed along to and if anyone else was involved.

Andrew put his game face on and walked into the conference room. He took a seat across form Christina and slowly placed a file in front of him on the table. He set there staring at her for what seemed like forever to her without saying a word to her. "As you have been informed my mate and I have been running background and security checks on everyone who is associated with Mr. Black or his family and we have a couple of issues we need to have clarified." Andrew said in a neutral tone.

"I will be glad to help set your mind at ease Mr. Barnes. Please feel free to ask me anything," Christina nervously offered.

Andrew looked at his watch and frowned. "I was going to play games with you but I just don't have the time today. Here is my first question what did you fax to Holiday Inn Express on the date that is indicated on the paper here?" Andrew asked as he handed her the paper.

Christina paled even more as she looked at the date and time. How did they find out she wondered? "I... I am sorry but I do recall that was a long time ago." Christina nervously responded.

"Christina, if that is true why are you suddenly afraid," Andrew asked as he sniffed the air. He smiled evilly as he continued in a hypnotic voice, "More like petrified, it smells so delicious."

Christina tried to shrink farther into the chair. She was almost paralyzed with fear and she thought that Andrew was losing control. Andrew allowed his baser half come forward and started to transfer. His eyes went to black lifeless orbs as his facial skin start to get a grey hue as it drew up and his lips thinned out making his fangs seem even larger than they were. "My baser half wants out and I am having trouble controlling him he wants revenge for the damage you caused to his mate. Now tell me the truth or I will let him have at you," Andrew said in a strained tone as he did, he mentally said, "Amelia I am in full control so please do not worry or let anyone else come in here yet"

Kirk started for the door to get into the room with Andrew and Christina when Amelia grabbed his arm and requested," Kirk please wait Andrew is in full control he is just trying to force her to confess."

Andrew flew across the table, grabbed Christina by the neck and slammed her into the wall his eyes were now lifeless orbs. His nails were imbedded into her neck and he applied enough pressure to make her very uncomfortable but not enough to do any real damage. "Tell me now or I will rip you apart a piece at a time." He threatened.

"I am sorry I didn't know he was going to try to kill her. Please forgive me all Amsu told me was to forward the file on Amanda and you so that Antonio Munoz could avoid you two." Christina pleaded.

Andrew knew she wasn't totally honest but he had what he needed for now. He let her fall to the floor where she curled up in a ball and hugged herself. "I will finish interrogating you after I am done with my appointment. I would suggest that you decide to cooperate fully with me if you don't it will get very painful very quickly." Andrew threatened in a cold tone.

Andrew then picked her up from the floor and shoved her towards the door. A moment later kirk walked in and grabbed her by the back of her neck. "What do you want me to do with her?" He asked.

"Please put her in a cell and chain her to the wall I want two guards on her at all times. She is to have no visitors," Andrew requested firmly.

Kirk glanced at Emma and saw her nod. He then lead Christina to a holding cell and chained her up as ordered. Meanwhile Andrew and Amelia quickly went and got dressed to go to Sanguinem and meet with Sam's friend. They arrived at the club around Seven forty-five and were shown right to the VIP room. Charles, Susan, Sam and Cindy were waiting for them. The two of them greeted the others warmly. "Sorry, we were running close but we had to conduct an interview with Ms. Morehouse," Amelia said casually.

"Was Christina able to satisfy your concerns?" Susan asked out of curiosity. She was sure whatever they thought they had found was either a mistake or a misunderstanding, she had known Christina for almost seventy years and had never had cause to doubt her.

"She is as guilty as all hell. She was the one who passed on our files to Munoz." Andrew responded with a snarl.

Susan was surprised but hid it well she managed to keep her expression neutral. The only sign that Charles was affected by Andrew proclamation was a slight darkening of his eyes. "How do you know she was the one who sent the information to him?" Charles asked his voice tightly controlled.

"The fax came from her desk and Andrew scared her into admitting her involvement. She claimed that she didn't know he was going to kill us. Once we are done here we will finish interrogating her and see how much damage she has done," Amelia replied with a bit of anger in her voice.

About that, time Helen and David was lead into the room and introductions were made. Cindy Susan and Helen moved off to get to know each other since David didn't want Helen involved in this conversation. He hoped her lack of knowledge would help to keep her safe.

"Sam I am sorry I had to cut you off so abruptly but if anyone overheard your question it could have been dangerous for all of us. Someone in the federal government wants to keep a tight lid on this. All of the evidence including the bodies has been seized and everyone with any knowledge was given the national security speech along with given a comprehensive list of friends and family as an implied threat if we talked," David explained.

"David are you and Helen safe?" Sam asked concerned for his friend.

"I'm not sure I am doing everything I can to protect Helen. I think I am already on their radar because I questioned the legality of what they were doing and it was quickly explained that national security trumped my legality arguments and if I persisted I would be taken into custody and held for security of the United States." David nervously answered.

There was a knock on the door and Paul Ryrie entered. He bowed slightly and waited until Charles acknowledged him. "What do you need Paul?" Charles asked.

"I apologize for disturbing you sir but there is something that you need to be aware of, Mr. Black," Paul whispered to Charles leaning in close.

"You can speak freely Paul." Charles said.

"Sir we have humans that have just entered the club they look like feds and are asking for the owner. What do you want me to do?" Paul asked.

"Have security stand-by. I will meet them in the conference room in a couple minutes." Charles ordered. He then addressed the others in the room, "Susan please see to our guest while Amelia, Andrew and I take care of the feds. Amelia I may have need your abilities with these gentlemen."

"Love I need you to convince David and Helen to allow us to send them to a place of safety so we can protect them. It is our fault that he is in danger," Charles telepathically said as he was addressing the others.

"I will do my best love. Should I alert Emma and have her get everyone else ready to leave?" Susan responded with her mind.

"I do not think it is necessary yet but have Paul get one of the vans ready to go encase we need to make a quick exit," Charles requested finishing the telepathic communication.

"Andrew are you and Amelia armed?" Charles asked.

"No we didn't think we would need to be. I hope that wasn't a mistake," Andrew replied calmly.

"No, if you were armed I was going to ask that you give your weapons to one of the security personnel," Charles replied quietly.

"We rarely carry anymore between Amelia's and my ability guns are almost useless." Andrew replied confidently.

"While that is most likely true just remember that becoming overly depended on your abilities can get you in trouble. Remember what happened when Amelia tried to erase Catherine's mind. I guess what I am trying to say is to keep your options open and don't get so set in the way you do things that it bites you in the ass," Charles advised seriously. He chuckled as he continued, "Besides my mate would be highly pissed at me if I let something happened to you all."

The three friends entered the office and Charles took a seat at the head of the table. Amelia was seated to his left and Andrew was to his right. The two feds walked into the office and stood at the other end of the table. "I am special agent Mathews and this is Agent Thomas of the FBI," Said Agent Mathews smugly.

"I am Charles Black the owner of this club and these are two of my associates Amelia and Andrew Barnes. They are members of my staff and Ms. Barnes will be acting as my legal counsel. Now how may I assist you gentleman?" Charles replied coldly not in the least intimidated by the two feds in front of him.

Amelia upon seeing Agent Thomas stiffened slightly but enough that both Andrew and Charles immediately noticed. "He knows me from when I was in the agency he was a junior agent assigned to the team that stopped the attack on Pearl." Amelia mental said to Andrew.

Andrew forced himself not to react to what Amelia had just told him. They watched as Agent Thomas stared at Amelia for a few seconds more then slowly moved his hand towards his weapon. "You are Special Agent Amelia Hensley but you are supposed to be dead."

Agent Thomas nervously announced. His eyes filled with terror as he started to draw his weapon.

Agent Mathews immediately went for his weapon he had worked with Jerry Thomas to know he was a good agent with a level head and if he said he knew this woman and she was supposed to be dead. He was going to take them all into custody until this mess could be hashed out.

Amelia immediately locked eyes with the two agents and took control of them. "You will stay your weapons and not move until I tell you to." Amelia ordered.

Both of the agents stopped going for their weapons and stood perfectly still awaiting further orders. Everyone could see and smell the fear emanating from the two of them. The four security men that were outside of the door came rushing into the room. Charles raised his hand indicating for them to stop.

"You will answer my questions honestly and will not hold anything back do you understand?" Amelia demanded.

"Yes mam." Agent Mathews replied immediately.

"I understand." Agent Thomas replied after a brief pause during which Amelia gave him a slight push with her abilities.

"Why are you here?" Amelia started the interrogation. The agents answered each of questions quickly and honestly. After thirty minutes of her interrogating them, she had managed to find out all that, they had known and that they were going to take Sam, David, Cindy and Helen into custody and deliver them to the Langley. She also found out that all of the information and evidence that was collected from the bombing was turned over to them. Amelia had made them both give her their username and password for the FBI and DOJ computer systems. Amelia then used her compulsion to have them keep her abreast of any information they find out relative to the case. She order them to remember that they searched the club from top to bottom and didn't find their suspects here and that owner and staff of the club were cooperative. Amelia made sure that they understood her instructions then turn them over to Charles so he could get them the hell out of the club.

"Thank you for your cooperation, Mr. Black," Agent Mathews said offering his hand.

"Glad we could assist you Agent Mathews. If I can be of any future assistance please feel free to call me." Charles shook the offered hand then handed him his card. He continued, "My personal cell number is on the back."

He then shook Agent Thomas's hand as he escorted the two of them out the door. Andrew and Amelia were standing in shadows in case something went wrong. Once the two agents left, Charles called the other enforcers to inform them about federal investigation. He had requested Amelia and Andrew to help Susan get Sam, David, and their wives to safety. They were going to Gloria's land in Scotland. The land was secluded and was outside of the United States Jurisdiction.

Andrew and Amelia returned to finish their interrogation of Christina. She wanted to make a deal she would cooperate fully if they would guarantee that she wouldn't be encased in concrete. Andrew wasn't inclined to give into her request but Amelia pointed out during their mental debate that it would far easier to retrieve the information they wanted with her cooperation. Emma and Susan both agreed with Amelia and since they had, no intention of encasing her anyhow quickly agreed.

Christina provided them with a complete list of everything she had passed onto Amsu .She had also given them all of her drop points and list of her contacts. She told them that Erik Ferranti was her intermediary. She claimed to have evidence that Erik was the one who found and recruited Alex Maslin. Amsu had convinced him that Charles had ordered his parents deaths. Christina had arranged for the press to be there. She had even hedged her bets by tell Catherine about the big sale at the baby store in the mall. Erik procured the bomb that Alex had used at the mall to kill Kirk and Linda. The original plan was to kill Emma hoping to expose vampires to humans. Amsu was sure if the humans found out about vampires they would restart the witch-hunts of old forcing vampires to have to defend themselves.

When asked why she would help with such a horrendous plan she casually said it was the millions she was promised. She had thought that she was too smart to be caught. Even when someone would notice her sending information to Amsu, she was just sending a report to Amsu for Charles, Emma or Neil and no one would question it. She didn't know where Amsu was or what he was planning to do. Christina asked what would happen to her and Andrew gladly informed her that she would have to face Charles and he most likely order her put to death. Andrew stated that he would like to be able to select her punishment because he would just lock her in a room and throw away the key. That is when Christina realized she had not escaped a slow painful death just changed the circumstances and she finally showed some remorse not for her actions but for her fate. Amelia did read her mind and made sure to scan all of her memories so she could be sure that Christina hadn't lied to them. Once they were done with their interrogation Emma ordered that Christina be placed in a secured cell, she was to be stripped naked and chained so that she couldn't hurt herself or escape. Lastly, there was to be a minimum of four guards on her at all times.

Amelia Called Charles and had him and Susan come join them for a full briefing on they had found out. Once the two of them had arrived, Andrew and she gave them a full report. Both Charles and Susan were beyond pissed once they found out who the target of the attack was both of them wanted to tear her to piece right then but Andrew suggested they wait until they had talked to the other enforcers. He rightly pointed out that they may want the option of talking to Christina themselves. Charles and Susan both reluctantly agreed to wait.

Charles went to deal with the other enforcers while Susan talked with Andrew and Amelia about how best to deal with Erik Ferranti. No one cares about Erik but Misha and her parents were old friends and allies. Misha unlike Erik would most likely go rogue if Erik were killed. Amelia suggested that perhaps they should talk to Misha family and try to come up with an agreement on how best protect Misha from Erik's guilt and punishment.

"The question is does anyone know where Erik relocated to?" Emma asked.

"They are in a hotel in Wilmington. Anatoly had asked your father if he would request you to reconsider allowing Erik to stay in the area for Misha sake. Your father agreed to talk to you but wanted to give you a couple days to cool off." Susan explained. After seeing Emma's face she added, "I was there and your father firmly stated that it was totally up to you and the only reason he would even ask was because of the respect he held for Anatoly and Faina."

Emma relaxed after she had gotten over the initial shock of her father overriding her without talking to her she did admit to herself that she would of did the same thing. "Amelia and Andrew do you think you two could go fetch Erik and drag his ass back to me. Please invite Misha here as my guest." Emma asked sweetly.

"Be our pleasure." The two of them said in unison. Susan handed them a slip of paper with the address and room number of the motel where the two of them were staying. They headed to where the Hummer was parked since they hadn't had a chance to go buy a new vehicle yet. When they got to the garage, Thomas was there waiting for them. He handed Andrew a couple sets of restraints and a gun for each of them.

Andrew programed the address into the GPS unit and the two of them headed towards their destination. The trip took them just over two hours. The hotel was extravagant to say the least Andrew was sure that Erik would insist on the presidential suite. "Andrew, how are we going to work this?" Amelia asked.

"I can think of a couple ways first we go in and you use your wonderful abilities to convince the man behind the desk that we are feds and we are looking for Erik in connection with a case," Andrew replied.

"While I like that way it isn't very discrete and may cause Charles and Susan's friends some embarrassment." Amelia said interrupting Andrew.

"True, then I guess you will have to use your abilities to convince the man behind the desk to give you there room number. Then we will give him the option of surrendering and walking out with his dignity intact or being handcuffed and marched through the hotel in front of everyone." Andrew finished his reply.

Amelia and Andrew walked to the front desk and Amelia quickly seized control of the woman behind the desk. Within a couple of minutes, Andrew and Amelia had the information they needed and a key to Erik's room. They took the elevator to the suite. Both Andrew and Amelia carefully shielded themselves so that Erik wouldn't pick up that they were vampires. Once they got to Erik and Misha's suite. They knocked and waited for someone to answer the door. Erik opened the door complaining that it had taken to long for room service he had ordered. He got the surprise of his life when Andrew rushed him and had him pinned on the floor. Misha seeing her mate was in trouble; quickly attempted to attack Andrew but was intercepted by Amelia. Amelia gently restrained Misha as she explained they were sent by Susan Dorchester to take Erik into custody.

Andrew handcuffed Erik and set him on the floor. He then went and closed the door to the suite while

Amelia calmed Misha down. Erik struggled against the restraints to no avail while demanding to know the meaning of this. He promised Andrew that he would have his head if he didn't release him. Misha begged to know what was going on she was more than a little concerned that Susan had ordered Erik to be taken into custody. "Would you please tell me what is going on?" Misha pleaded as tears started running down the sides of her face.

"Your mate plotted with others to assassinate Emma Black and to expose vampires to humans. He was one of the people behind the attack at the mall." Amelia gently explained as she held Misha's hand.

"How could you?" Misha demanded angrily. She stared at Erik who had a smug look on his face.

"If I did do this there is nothing they can do to me because of you and your family. Don't worry we will come out of this just fine," Erik replied with a large grin on his face.

"Erik do you really think just because you are mated to me will protect you this time. Did you try to kill Emma?" Misha asked in horror.

"They can't prove anything, there is no evidence," Erik stated avoiding her question.

Misha just bowed her head and cried. She knew her mate was a bastard and only loved money but she never thought he would destroy her in this way. This could destroy her family; Charles was well within his rights to order not only Erik and her to be put to death but also her parents. "What will Charles do to us?" Misha whispered the question softly in between sobs.

"We are to take him into custody and return him to Philly for questioning. We were requested to ask you to join us please as Emma guest." Andrew responded honestly.

"What is Charles planning to do with my parents?" Misha queried nervously.

"The last we heard he was going to talk to them and let them know what was going on and make sure that the three of you were kept safe." Andrew answered her question trying to reassure her.

Misha relaxed after hearing Andrew's answers. She could sense no deception in his voice and somehow seeing how concern he was for her comfort reassured her. She studied the two of them there was something familiar about Andrew even though she had never meant him. Misha was sure that they were young but she could sense their strength. She was trying to figure out how she knew Andrew. Amelia noticed that Misha had more than a passing interest in her mate but determined it was not romantically motivated so she would tolerate it.

Andrew called Emma and let her know they had Erik in custody and were going to be returning with him shortly. He had just hung up the phone when there was a knock at the door. They all sensed the visitor was a vampire. Erik looked relieved and Amelia sensed he was about to yell out for help so she quickly took control of Erik's mind ordering him to remain quiet. "Who is it?" Misha asked when Andrew prompted her.

Amelia quickly read Erik's mind and found out that the vampire at the door was an assassin sent here to kill Misha and help Erik to escape. Erik had made killing her part of the deal when he agreed to help Amsu. "Andrew he is here to kill Misha." Amelia quickly warned Andrew through their bound.

"I am friend of Erik's. He called me and asked me to stop by," The vampire replied in a soothing voice.

"He is in the bedroom, just a minute while I get him." Misha replied trying to hide the nervousness in her voice.

Andrew sent Misha to the bedroom. Amelia realized the vampire in the hall had no idea that Andrew and her were there and quickly informed Andrew of that fact through their link. Andrew wondered why that was but decided to talk to Charles or Susan later. Andrew moved to beside the door and turned invisible hoping to get an advantage. He told Amelia that he would tackle the vampire at the door and try to give her the opportunity to take control of the vampires mind. Andrew really wanted him alive. Once Andrew was in place Amelia quickly ripped off Erik's shirt and unbuckled the belt on his pants. Then she had him take off his shoes and socks, before he answered the door. As soon as he opened the door, the assassin stabbed him in the chest with a large Bowie style knife narrowing missing his heart. Andrew seeing this happen quickly grabbed the vampires arm and forced him to let go of the knife breaking the arm in the process. The vampiric assassin was surprised and before the assassin could recover, Andrew unleashed a couple powerful blows that dazed him just before he could recover Andrew had slammed the assassin to the floor. The assassin tried to struggle against Andrew, but was at a disadvantage because of his broken arm and Andrew quickly subdued him and used the other set of cuffs they had been given to restrain him not caring about the other vampire's broken arm.

While Andrew was, busy with the vampire that had attacked Erik. Amelia went to assist Erik. She quickly dragged him out of the way and checked him over. The wound was far from fatal but she imagined it was painful. She went to quickly retrieved a couple of towels from the bathroom and by the time she had returned Andrew had the other vampire in custody and was trying to keep a very distraught Misha calmed and away from her mate so that Amelia would be able to tend to him.

Amelia looked into Misha's eyes as she returned to aid Erik and forced her to calm down. Misha was stunned how easily Amelia was able to circumvent her mental defenses and push into her mind. It fascinated and worried her at the same time. Andrew released Misha now that she was calmed and she set down on the couch trying to stay out of their way. She nervously watched as Amelia treated her mates wounds.

Amelia quickly removed the knife from Erik's chest and covered the wound with the towels applying pressure to lessen his loss of blood. Andrew had found ten units of blood and handed Amelia a couple of them to feed to Erik once his wound was sealed. Amelia let Erik drink the two units of blood she knew that he wanted and most likely needed more to regain his strength but she decided that it was better to keep him weakened. Amelia locked eyes with the assassin and ordered him not to move or talk until she ordered him to then cared for his broken arm.

While Amelia tended to her charges, Andrew started get rid of any evidence of the altercation thankfully there had no broken furniture to hid or replace. After he was done with that, he gathered up the anything that may look suspicious like empty blood bags or the blood soaked towels. Andrew made sure that Erik's laptop and files were packed to go with them. They would have another team return in the morning to go over the room with a fine toothcomb looking for anything that Amelia and Andrew may had missed. Andrew led the group out to the vehicles just in case one of their prisoners tried anything but thanks to Amelia's abilities the two of them obediently followed the directions they were given. Andrew restrained the two prisoners in the back most seats. Amelia and Misha were seated in middle seats and Andrew was driving. The trip was uneventful. Once they arrived at the building where they all were staying, the two prisoners were taken to holding cells and Misha was shown to a guest room. Amelia and Andrew called it a night after giving Charles, Emma, and Susan a quick rundown of the events that had happened before heading to clean up and catch a few hours of shuteye.

The next morning Amelia and Andrew were introduced to Anatoly and Faina Aaronic. They had been updated about the previous day's events. The only thing Amelia and Andrew had not disclosed as of yet was the fact that the assassin target was Misha, Amelia wanted a chance to confirm that fact before she deliver that kind of devastating news. Charles and Anatoly were going to try to come up with a way to insulate Misha so that Erik could be punished without harming Misha. While Susan and Faina were going to try to help Misha to regain the strength, she once possessed.

Amelia and Andrew quickly excused themselves so they could go interrogate Erik and their mystery guest. The two of them had been promoted to head of security for all of the black's interest without them even being aware of it. Faina and Susan followed the two of them out. "Excuse me," Faina called out. She waited until Both Andrew and Amelia had turn to face her before continuing, "I do not mean to be forward but what are the two of you holding back. Please don't try to hide it, I can sense that you are holding back and it has to do with my daughter."

"Ms. Aaronic we left no facts out of our report. I am hesitant about passing on unsubstantiated information that could do more harm than good." Andrew explained in a cool almost indifferent tone.

"Love she is just concerned for her daughter. Is everything all right with you? You seem a bit edgy." Amelia telepathically said her mental voice full of concern.

"I am ok but you are right something has me a bit on edge." Andrew replied to Amelia with his mind as he said in a softer tone, "Ms. Aaronic I am sorry if I seem a bit short with you I am just bit on edge. My mate sensed that the unidentified vampire was there to kill your daughter but we want to get all of the facts before we say something wrong."

"You think that Erik wanted my daughter killed?" Faina asked shocked and horrified.

"That is what we are going to find out Ms. Aaronic and I promise we will let you and your husband know what we find out. Andrew responded in a reassuring tone.

Andrew asked the guards to bring in Erik first. Andrew and Amelia agreed Erik would be the easier one to interrogate. A shackled Erik was led into the interrogation room. He wore a smug smile on his face and confidently set in the chair acting as if he was going to business lunch and not an interrogation that could garner him a death sentence.

"I take it you know I was helping Amsu and want to know what I told him." Erik smugly said.

"So you admit to treason and attempting to expose vampires to the humans." Amelia asked surprised at his admission.

"I think it was a bit more than an attempt. However, yeay I do, after all it isn't like you can do anything more than lock me up. If you kill me poor little Misha would be destroyed," Erik stated with a mixture of distain and arrogance.

"You do realize there are worse things than dying," Andrew threatened.

"That may well be true but I will just open my mind to Misha to make sure she feels everything I do. How long do you think it will take her to lose what little bit of sanity she has the poor weak pathetic creature she is." Erik taunted never changing his smug smile.

Andrew's eyes flashed in anger, he couldn't comprehend not doing everything in his power to protect his mate, and this piece of shit was using his mate as a shield. Before Amelia could react, Andrew lashed out with his telekinetic abilities. He threw Erik across the room he went through the wallboard and smashed into the brick wall behind it. Andrew had managed to turn right shoulder and upper arm into a maraca. The guards stationed outside of the room came pouring in to see what the loud crashing sound was while Amelia quickly wrapped her arms around Andrew while used her mind to attempt to settle him down and to her surprise, Andrew was in full control of himself.

"I bet you won't be so smug now," Andrew said with a smug smile of his own. He then directed the guards to reseat Erik in his chair and leave the room. Unfortunately, for Erik there was no Miranda Rights to protect him from being tortured. Erik was reseated in the chair and the guards left the room. Erik looked at Andrew with more than a bit of fear in his eyes waiting for Andrew to speak.

"Erik you think that you can hide behind your mate and will be safe, however I am sure that if I ask real nice my lovely mate will be most glad to use her mind to shield your mate from you then I can do most anything except kill you." Andrew stated in a soft but firm tone.

"Andrew I am not sure I can do that." Amelia quickly told Andrew with her mind while keeping her expression carefully neutral.

"He doesn't need to know that." Andrew replied mentally while he was studying Erik.

Erik tried to gauge if Andrew was serious or not but decided not to challenge him. He wondered if he had gone too far this time. Misha had always been his get out of jail free card even when he had the occasional run in with the Blacks but it wasn't protecting him this time. As he was setting there, he became aware of a presence in his mind and tried to force it out of his mind unsuccessfully.

Amelia wanted the complete story and wasn't willing to play anymore games with him no matter how much fun her mate was having decided to use Erik moment of indecision to her advantage and sneak into his mind. When she had tried to slip in earlier, she had meant a wall of defenses and she was unwilling to risk damaging Misha well-being decided to wait and let Andrew take the lead. Now that his defenses were done, she had managed to push through his defenses and by the time, Erik had realized she had breached his shield, she had him. She ordered Erik to lower his defenses and allow her complete access to his mind, which he reluctantly allowed. Amelia quickly and non-to gently tore through his memories she had ordered him to block off his link with his mate to protect her. Amelia was sickened by some of the plans he had for his mate and her family. He was the one who had insisted that Amsu have his mate and her family killed as part of his compensation for helping Amsu with his plans. Amelia now knew that Amsu had been planning to cause a war between the vampires for almost a quarter of a century according to Erik's memories.

Andrew was just about to restart the interrogation when he realized that Amelia had taken control of Erik's mind and was in the process of reading his mind. He could see the pain on Erik's face and was enjoying watching his lovely mate rip though Erik's mind. He wondered whether Amelia would leave Erik's mind intact or would he wind up a breathing husk like Victor Stone. He stood ready just in case Erik broke her control but knowing that normally once Amelia had someone, they were hers for as long as she wanted them. Once Amelia was done, he escorted Erik to his cell with orders to have him chained to the wall and watched by no less than two guards at all times. Andrew decided to take a break to give Amelia a chance to regain her strength he could feel her weariness through their bound.

Amelia rested while Andrew made the arraignments to have Erik properly detained and watched. Erik had resisted her mental probes and the resulting battle had tired her. She needed a few minutes to regain her strength in order to be able to assist in the next interrogation. She knew that Faina Aaronic would be demanding to know what they had found out but she wanted to let Charles or Susan decide how much to tell her and her husband. She picked up the phone, called Charles, and asked him to come down to the interrogation room without his guest so she could go over what she found out. Just as she hung up the phone, Andrew returned and she filled him in on what she had found out from also letting him know she had requested Charles to join them alone. While the two of them waited, she wondered who the Aaronic were, as Charles seemed to hold the family in high regard and went out of his way to accommodate them.

CHAPTER 2

***

A short time later Charles joined, the two of them in the interrogation room to hear the report of Erik's interrogation. As Charles listened to the report he could hardly believe just how freely Erik used his mate to shield his wrong doings he almost didn't want to believe that Erik not only threatened to allow Misha to be harmed but had actually threatened to cause harm to her himself. Charles could not help to wonder just what kind of monster he was. After Amelia finished giving Charles the report, he requested that they share in the information with Faina and Anatoly. As the three of them were leaving the room, Charles' cell started to ring. Charles waved them to go on. "How in the hell did it happen?" Andrew and Amelia heard Charles shout into the phone.

Charles listened, as the other person must have spoken. "I will have my investigators out there as soon as possible... No, you don't know them but they are very good at their job... I will send Gloria along with them is that acceptable? ... I don't wish to discuss this on an unsecure line. I will call you back soon." Charles ended the phone call his rage barely contained. He mentally sent Susan a brief synopsis of the telephone conversation he had just had and asked that Gloria and her join him in his office in ten minutes. He then called his private jet and put it on stand-by telling them to ready to fly in thirty minutes. When they asked, where they would be going he answered San Diego, California and make arraignments to have rental vehicles.

Charles started to go ask Andrew and Amelia to join him when his phone rang again. He was slightly surprised at the identity of the caller Walter Astin. "Hello Walter, what can I do for you?" Charles answered the phone in a business like tone.

"First of let me express my sincere regrets. I tried to get men there to assist your people but they got there too late. I didn't realize it was a problem until my man that was monitoring your teams failed to check in. Fortunately, he was just disabled and not killed so I will make sure he is available to answer any question your team has I would also like to offer my full assistance in this matter. I have already provided your people here with three vehicles equipped and stocked for your investigators and if you wish I will provide Marsha as a liaison and three drivers that know the area." Astin offered.

Charles was surprised by Astin's offer he hadn't expected such a generous offer. If Astin was going to support him, it would make the job of locating who was responsible much easier. "Thank you Walter I appreciate and accept your offer. May I request one last thing from you? A copy of any information that you have already gathered so my team can review it on the trip out." Charles replied grateful for his help.

"I will be glad to fax it to you just give me the number and I have sealed off the scene until your people arrive also I have the victim's body. Is it true .that it is the family of one of your people?" Astin replied

"Yes do you recall the hearing about the two people that were turned by diamond?" Charles asked.

Yes, one was a homicide cop Andrew Martin and the other was a federal agent named Amelia something or other. Is it true that they killed her while still being human?" Astin answered curious to see where this was going.

"Yes Andrew killed Diamond while he was still human. It is his ex-wife, child and her new husband. Andrew and his mate Amelia along with Gloria will be leading the investigation. Before you ask yes the two of them are young but they are very good at this type of work." Charles explained earnestly.

"Charles are you sure it is a good idea to have Andrew involved in this matter he may be too close to this to think objectively. I mean after all it is his child that is missing." Astin replied concerned. He knew that Charles normally was good at staying objective but he had to wonder about Charles judgment in this case.

"I appreciate your concern but I can think of no better people to have on the case and I am confident that as long as Amelia is with him he will be able to control himself. I have never seen a mating bond quite like theirs they seem to balance each other perfectly. Secondly one of the reasons I am sending Gloria along with them is to monitor the two of them and act as a safety in case I am mistaken," Charles answered. He was positive that Andrew would have no trouble containing himself but wanted Gloria there in case he was mistaken.

"Ok Charles then I am looking forward to meeting the two of them and renewing my friendship with Gloria. O' by the way I understand congratulation are in order. Please extend them to your wonderful mate." Astin finished with a couple less important items they needed to discuss and hung up right after Charles gave him the fax number.

Charles went to his office and found Susan and Gloria waiting for him he quickly explained to Gloria what had happened in California and what he needed her to do. She quickly agreed to help in whatever way she could and would try to help keep Andrew calm. All three of them knew that if Andrew found Amsu all bets were off and he and Amelia would Attack him on sight no matter what they promised. Charles made Gloria promise to get away from them and call for back --up to hopefully save their friends they all knew that Andrew and Amelia were no match for Amsu and unless he was toying with them their lives would be over quickly.

After Charles was satisfied with everything he went over with Gloria, he requested that Amelia, Emma, Andrew and Neil to join them in the office he hoped that all of them being there would help Andrew to keep control of his baser self. Emma and Neil enter his office almost immediately followed by Neil and a very pregnant Catherine. Scott was at work and wouldn't be home for a few hours. "Catherine it may be better if you weren't in here when I talk to Andrew." Charles suggested worried that if Andrew reacted badly he could inadvertently hurt the baby or Catherine.

"Charles, Andrew would never hurt me or my child. You know this," Catherine argued.

"Catherine I didn't mean he would lash out against you I meant he may lose control of his powers and lash out with them." Charles explained.

"Hun she will be a reminder to Andrew to stay in control. I think you should let her stay." Susan reasoned hoping to prevent an argument.

Charles nodded his acquiesce and hoped that Susan was right. A couple moments later Andrew and Amelia came through the door and were a bit surprised to see everyone there. "What's up?" Andrew asked while smiling. He quickly lost his smile when he saw Charles expression. Andrew immediately went on alert followed very quickly by Amelia.

"Andrew it is no immediate threat I just have some bad news to relay to you and I need you to remain as calm as possible. Last night your ex-wife Shannon was attacked and killed in her home. We haven't been able to locate your son or Tony as of yet. Andrew I cannot tell you how sorry I am. I had two teams on them at all times but whoever did this managed to kill all of the men I had on them." Charles said sincerely.

Andrew set down heavily on the edge of the coach by him and Amelia quickly wrapped her arms around him and pulled his head to her chest. Andrew started to shake as tears of rage and sorrow started to flow. He closed his eyes, and fought for control knowing that the time to grieve would come; but first he had to keep his mind focused so that he could find his son and then once he was safe he would find the person or persons who had done this and they would pay dearly very dearly. "Charles I need all information you have so far and how soon can we get a plane to San Diego and we will need to know the location of the blood suppliers by Solana Beach area." Andrew quietly queried.

Everyone was surprised how calmly Andrew had taken the news Charles most of all. Charles study Andrew for a few minutes wondering if he was in shock or denial but his words and action seemed to suggest other wise . "Andrew slow down a moment," Charles said then paused for a couple of seconds to make sure he had Andrew's attention. Once he saw that he did he continued, "I have my jet on stand-by at Philadelphia International Airport. Gloria will be going with you to help with the search. Walter Astin has put his lead investigator Marsha Chids at your disposal. He also will be providing you with the use of vehicles and drivers. Most importantly, he has placed his resources at your disposal."

"Andrew I know this is hard but I need your word that you will conducted this as an investigation with the goal of retrieving your son and Tony if he is still alive and not a witch-hunt. I want the ones who are responsible for this as much if not more than you do." Charles finished hoping that his words would sink in.

"Charles I would be lying if I said I didn't want to avenge my ex-wife, son and Tony but I swear this to you my son comes first once I have him safe then I will worry about seeking those who perpetrated this and making them sorry they were ever born " Andrew replied keeping his voice tightly controlled.

"Andrew I know you don't like the political arena but I need you to try to be as diplomatic as you can when dealing with Astin or his people. His cooperation will make your job a lot easier." Charles explained.

"I will be as diplomatic as I can." Andrew promised.

"Ok then go pack and get ready to go Susan and I will be taking the three of you to the airport. I would suggest you drink a couple units of blood," Charles suggested. He then called to make arraignment for one of the minivans.

The ride to the airport was somber to say the least hardly any words were spoken and the few that were was just to pass on information the three of them would need to be able to fulfill their assignment. Andrew was introspective and showed almost none of his normal personality. Susan was concerned for her young friend and hoped that Amelia would be able to keep Andrew from allowing his baser side to gain control.

The three of them boarded one of Charles' private jets and after takeoff, the three friends gathered around one of the conference tables and started to go over the information that Walter Astin had sent them. Her body had been found in the family room of the home that was owned by her and her husband. The report stated that the vampires that were guarding the Andrew's family were beheaded quickly before at least five vampires entered the residence and were inside approximately thirty minutes. The human female was killed while the human male and child was taken with the vampires in question.

The neat report was the autopsy report for Shannon. It stated that the victim had been repeatedly raped and beaten before she was killed. It also stated that at least three different vampires had drained her; she had bite marks on both wrists in addition to her neck. The final insult was the removal of her heart and brain.

After reading all of the information they had available the three of them decided as long as it was acceptable to Walter Astin Amelia would go interview the vampire that had been responsible for keeping an eye on Charles security teams while Gloria and Andrew would go the house where Shannon was killed and see if they could pick-up anything. Gloria suggested that the three of them rest until they landed so that they would all have fresh minds. Andrew went to a window seat to watch the scenery. He didn't even realize he had dozed off until he was woken up by Amelia telling him they would be landing soon.

About thirty minutes later the three friends were meant by Walter Astin his mate Elaine and Marsha Hobes. After introductions and greeting were made Walter asked," Where would you like to begin?"

"I would like for Gloria and myself to investigate the crime scene while Amelia interviews the investigator who was subdued by the perpetrators of the attack." Andrew replied keeping his tone business like.

"Richard Fenton the investigator is waiting for you in the van I thought it may help speed up the process. I have six teams out searching for your son and Tony. If I can be of any assistance please call me, my personal cell number is on the back of the card." Walter Astin explained as he handed Andrew his card.

"Thank you, Mr. Astin. I will keep you up to date on our progress," Andrew replied taking the card and then offering his hand.

"Please call me Walter. I have made arraignments for rooms for you, your mate, and Ms. Vegas. If there is nothing else, I can assist you with then I will leave you in the capable hands of Ms. Hobes." Walter said while shaking Andrew's hand. He then shook Amelia's hand and gave Gloria a friendly hug before leaving them with Marsha Hobes.

Marsha Led the group to the van that held Richard Fenton when Andrew first saw him, he was surprised he wasn't what Andrew was expecting. Richard Fenton was just over five feet tall with a slight build. Andrew doubted the he weighed one hundred pounds wet. Andrew noted that Richard reacted with humor as he watched Andrew assess him. Amelia had a similar reaction but was a bit better at hiding her surprise.

"The reaction that the two of you are having is exactly why I am normally excel at my job. Ms. Barnes, I understand that you have the ability to read memories." Richard said humor coloring his voice.

"I am sorry about our reaction, you weren't what we were expecting and yes I do have the ability to read memories," Amelia replied confirming what he had heard.

"Not to worry like I said I use my height or lack thereof to my advantage. No one seems to take note of me normally. The reason I had asked about your abilities is that I believe that the person who incapacitated me ordered me not to remember what I saw that night." Richard explained. He was hoping that the rumors he had heard about her abilities were true he was not happy that someone had managed to get the drop on him and then fuck with his head.

"If you wish I can try to search your memories and find out if they did anything to you," Amelia offered.

"Please, I want to remember. Just tell me what I need to do." Richard beseeched.

"Just relax and please lower you mental shield," Amelia instructed. She gave Richard a few moments to relax himself then locked her eyes with his and gently started to probe his memories. She scanned his memories looking for the ones from when he was incapacitated. After she found them, she could tell that someone had placed some form of a mental block so she decided to help him to overcome the block so he could recall the memories. She guided Richard around the mental block and allowed Richard to access the memories. After Amelia had guided him around the block, she mentally stepped back allowing him to take the lead. She would keep him on the task of bringing those memories forward and would watch them with him. She watched as he now recalled the events of the night in vivid detail. Richard had been keeping an eye on Charles people to one see if they were just watching a vampire's human family like Charles claimed and secondly in case they ran into any trouble so he could summon assistance if they ran into trouble. Walter felt it prudent to take these steps the last thing he needed was for a bunch of Charles' people to be killed after he had granted them safe passage.

The night had been long and boring and Richard was glad when Harry showed up an hour early to replace him. The two of them were talking when Richard felt the presence of another vampire but seeing that Harry hadn't reacted to her Richard thought it was just Ilesha Harry's mate. Richard knew that Harry would occasionally bring her along on long boring stakeouts. He didn't realize it wasn't her until he felt the prick of the needle piercing his skin then a slight burning sensation of the unknown drug they had given him. He knew that the scent was vaguely familiar but the drug took effect before he could identify whom she was. Even though he still couldn't identify it, he would recognize the scent if he ever smelled it again. Amelia made sure that Richard could access those memories and quickly removed herself from his mind. Amelia would be able to identify the female that had injected Richard by scent now. Marsha watched as Amelia probed Richard's mind she was surprised how much control Amelia seemed to have of her ability. The last time Walter had Keisha probe on of his investigator's mind it was to say very painful for him but Richard was totally relaxed and showed no signs of discomfort.

Amelia informed everyone what she had seen in Richards mind so the appropriate calls could be made in order to try to capture Harry so they could interrogate him. After she was done she set there for a few minutes with her eyes closed trying to regain her energy. Using this power still was a bit of a drain on her. This time was not as bad as the other times because Richard hadn't fought her. She could sense his apprehension when she first tried to enter so she waited until he was comfortable and relaxed before she entered his mind.

Richard was relaxing with his head against the headrest of the seat as he tried to identify the scent he now remembers, thanks to Amelia. He knew he had smelled it before but couldn't recall to whom the scent belonged. He knew he had meant the woman in question before, but couldn't for the life of him recall her so he figured it had to be in the distant past after all he had meant a lot of people since he was turned over eight hundred years ago. As he sat there, he wondered if Amelia could maybe help him to recall who this woman was. Noting that they were almost to their destination he decided he would ask her later on. "Ms. Barnes I cannot thank you enough for your help," Richard said as he bowed slightly.

"My pleasure I wish I could have identified that woman's scent. I know I have smelled it before." Amelia responded.

The van pulled up in front of Toni's and Shannon's home. Marsha led the others into the house and then stood out of the way to allow Andrew and Amelia to conduct their investigation. Gloria stood beside Marsha carefully watching Andrew for any signs he was losing control. Andrew and Amelia slowly circled the living room where the attack had taken place, looking for anything that the others may have missed. They couldn't find anything that the other team that went through her house had missed. Amelia was focused on trying to see what was going through the minds of the vampires who had done this horrendous act the trouble was they had left few clues that could help her. She noted for the apparent violence of the attack the room was remarkably undisturbed no overturned furniture or broken nick-knacks. There was very little blood only a couple small stains by where the body had laid. She went into the file and noticed from the autopsy report that Shannon hos no defensive wounds even though from the repost she had endured an extensive ante-mortem beating. The report had listed several broken ribs and her torso had extensive bruising.

Andrew wanted to see if his psychometry would work so he moved to where someone had outlined where the body had laid and placed his hand on the carpet. Immediately he had an image of Shannon frightened out her mind laying there while Toni in full vampiric mode violently raping her. Andrew watched in horror as the man he had trusted the safety of his ex-wife and child taking pleasure in hurting her he could see other vampires standing around the room but couldn't get a clear image of them. The image faded and then was replaced by the next image of Tony latched on to the side of Shannon's neck while two other vampires that Andrew didn't know were latched on to her wrist. Tears started to run down the sides of Andrew's face as he watched the woman that was the mother of his child die. He vowed that he would track each and every one of them down and feast on their blood.

Andrew knew that there were at least four other vampires in the room but they appeared a vague outlines one of which was directing things from a chair over by the fireplace. He quickly realized that Tony was a feral vampire, which meant that he had to be found and put down quickly. He slowly rose and stood there for a couple minutes fighting to regain the total control he needed, to be able to find his son. He felt Amelia's arms wrap around him form the back and felt as she laid her head in between his shoulders. "Love we will find him and we will also take care of those who a responsible for this," Amelia softly promised.

"It was Tony love he has been turned and he is feral. He was the one that raped and murdered Shannon," Andrew stated his voice choked with emotion. He was in such shock that he didn't even think that Amelia had already known because of their bond.

Both Marsha and Gloria were surprised by Andrew announcement that the husband had been the one who raped and killed her. Marsha reached for her cellphone and quickly dialed Walter's number if Andrew was correct and Toni had been turn into a feral vampire then Walter had to be informed immediately. While she waited for an answer, she wondered who was behind this attack and if it had anything to do with the attack on those vampires in Philadelphia. She had seen the reports on the cable news channel right after it had happened. She had heard a rumor that Amsu was behind it but once all of the publicity had died down the rumor mill quickly dried up. She was surprise when Elaine answered the cell. "Elaine is Walter available?" Marsha hurriedly asked.

"He is right here but his hands are occupied so I answered the phone. What 's up?" Elaine replied humor coloring her voice.

"Are you free to talk? The information is sensitive." Marsha inquires wanting to make sure that they were in an area where the conversation couldn't be over heard.

"I am in my office. Now what is going on," Walter demanded his displeasure evident in his tone. His hands had indeed been filled with his mate's luscious ass as she set on the edge of his desk while he was feasting on her. As he waited for Marsha to explain what she wanted he started to slide his rock hard member into Elaine's white-hot sheath. Even after being mated for over a century he still wanted her as much if not more than the night he saw her standing on the balcony of the Marquise hotel in May of Eighteen ninety six.

"Sorry but it seems we have a bigger issue than we first thought. The human male has been turned and is apparently feral," Marsha quickly explained. As she waited for a response, she heard a string of curses that would have made a sailor blush then the phone went quiet for a moment.

"How do you know he has been turned and he is feral?" Walter asked needing to know how she came by this information. He grimaced as he slid out of his mate;

unfortunately, this needed his undivided attention. Elaine gave him a sympathetic smile letting him know she understood.

"Andrew seems to have psychometry and claims he saw the attack when placed his hands on the carpet where the body was found," Marsha replied.

"Object read? Interesting. I will contact the search parties and make sure that they have this information then I will call the Ubertas Venator and get them mobilized. The last thing we need is a feral parvulus rampaging through the streets. Has anyone contacted Charles yet?" Walter asked as he was going over a mental checklist of what needed to be done. He would alert the local vampire establishments and hangouts. He was just about to call the head of the local Ubertas Venator when his phone rang.

"Hello Charles you called faster than I expected." Walter said with a touch of humor.

"Hello Walter. I know but I didn't want you to waste your time calling the Ubertas Venator. Gloria will hunt Tony down and I want to try to take him alive..." Charles started to explain.

"Why in the hell would you attempt that? You know that once a vampire has crossed over he cannot be brought back. He is just a dangerous rabid animal that needs to be put down," Walter Argued.

"I am not saying we won't put him down. I am hoping that Amelia may be able to pull some information from him that will lead us to the child." Charles finished explaining.

"I will agree as long as it doesn't endanger anyone and I also want to be kept in the loop and I mean I want updates as soon as you get them," Walter stated firmly.

"I agree to all of your terms. As far as the rogue vampire goes, I wouldn't expect you to endanger anyone life on a chance that we may get some information." Charles agreed thankful that Walter was being so reasonable.

Charles shared all of the information on the recent events starting with Amsu attempt on his daughter's life. He didn't include any assumptions as to let Walter draw his own conclusions in hopes of a fresh prospective from a neutral third party. After he had shared all of the pertinent information, Walter agreed that all of the recent attacks seemed related and promised to keep Charles updated on any new developments on his end. By the end of the call, the two of them had agreed to a tentative alliance.

Andrew moved to the chair, placed his hand on it, and saw the blurred image of a vampire he could sense he was old and seemed almost frail until he felt how powerful the vampire's mind was. Andrew felt a sense of dread coming from this vampire and as he watched him, direct the events of that evening, Andrew felt the oppressive air in the room that emanated from this vampire. He looked to the left of this vampire and saw Amsu standing there with a large smile on his face he heard him bragging about how this would hasten the war that was needed to bring the vampire race back to its former place of glory. Andrew refocused on the other vampire whomever he was he was malevolent. Andrew tried to make out any details he could about this new vampire but he couldn't make out any fine details; it was as if he was looking at an out of focus picture when he looked at the mysterious vampire even though the rest of the images were sharp and clear.

Andrew could sense that the mysterious vampire was almost bored; he seemed to be disinterested in the events unfolding before him even though he was the puppet master. Andrew could sense the vampire's only interest was the reward that he was promised. He suddenly had a flash of insight as to what the reward was and the bile started to rise from his stomach as his primal side came exploding forward.

Amelia was standing next to Andrew wondering what he was seeing in his images. She could feel his disgust and anger at the images he saw but she could tell he was in full control of himself. She sensed he was trying to probe deeper into what he was seeing when all of the sudden she felt his primal side come rushing forward.

His eyes darkened and he almost immediately transformed into his baser self. She quickly wrapped her arms around him and tried to push into his mind sending calming images to him however this time she was meeting a wall of resistance. The good thing was that she still had enough sway of him for the moment to keep him rooted where he was even though she could sense he wanted to run or possible outrun something. His thoughts were all over the place and for the first time since his change, she could sense gut wrenching fear from him.

Marsha was briefing Gloria on her conversation she had just had with Walter when they both felt Andrew baser side explode forward. Gloria grabbed Marsha and moved her outside of the house. "Amelia is going to need to get his undivided attention in order to try to talk him down." Gloria explained as she wondered what set Andrew off he had been showing excellent control even with the added stress of the murder of his ex-wife and the kidnapping of his son. She could only assume that he had seen something in his visions that had caused his loss of control and she prayed that it was not the death of his son.

Andrew struggled to maintain control as he felt Amelia's arms wrap around him. He could feel her attempt at calming him but even with her support he was losing control he desperately wanted to get his hands on the vampire he saw setting there Andrew wasn't sure how he knew his intentions but he did the bastard was going to take his son and make him his. He could see the perverted ideas he had in store for his son and he wouldn't allow it. The only thing that kept him from completely crossing over was that somewhere in the back of his mind he knew he had to remain calm in order to be able to track his son. That thought added to the combination of Amelia scent and the constant wave of her calming reassurance that they would find his son before it was too late gave Andrew the strength to bring his baser side back under control for now. As he calmed he picked upon final image it was the front of the hotel he staying at when this attack had happened.

While Amelia was holding on to her mate trying to calm him she started to pick up some very disturbing images from Andrew's mind at first she thought he was seeing what had happened to his child but after a few minutes she realized this was what one of the vampires was planning to do to his son. She knew she had to keep control of herself in spite of these sickening images or Andrew would lose what little control he had at the moment.

Andrew took about fifteen minutes to finally recompose himself afterward he explain what he had saw in his visions to the rest of the group. Gloria called Charles while Marsha contacted Walter and the both of them relayed the information to their respective leaders. Walter promised to contact all of the local vampire establishments and coven leaders to alert them to be on the lookout for the vampire that Andrew had described. Charles started calling the other enforcer hoping to get a lead on the identification of the new vampire.

After Andrew finished telling the others what he had learned he started to wonder how he had done never before had he been able to pick up intentions and thoughts it was always like watching a movie he could only hear what was being said. He realized whomever this new vampire was he was trying to bait him into a confrontation. Andrew relished the idea of getting his hands on this bastard. He would take great pleasure in ripping him into small pieces as he feasted on his blood.

As Andrew moved around the room he suddenly got this over whelming feeling of anger and something else he couldn't quite identify he hadn't realized he had placed his hand on the door back of sofa. Andrew could only pick up a partial image of what was going on and it didn't make a lot of sense. He could hear Amsu angrily stating he was betrayed by someone and that he would find a replacement. He heard Amsu promise that the replacement would be there by the end of the week then he turned to someone else and ordered that he find the bitch that had betrayed him and bring her head to him or it would be the person who he was speaking to head.

Andrew shared the images he had garnered with Amelia and his suspicions that the unknown vampire was trying to bait him into a confrontation. Amelia wasn't sure that it would be a good idea for just the two of them to confront him on their own. She could sense that he was old almost as old as Amsu and the two of them had yet to master their abilities. Andrew had trouble with controlling his pyro abilities. He could use them at will but the results varied; sometimes they would do exactly what he wanted and other times the fire would quickly get out of hand. The last time they had worked on his control he was just supposed to light a candle with them he would up igniting every burnable object in a spectacular fashion. Hell he even managed to cause the fire resistant wallboard to spontaneously combust. Thankfully, the fire suppression system kicked in and doused the flames before there was too much damage after that fiasco Charles thought it would be pertinent to forgo farther training until they could find a safer location. He had advised Andrew to use that ability only in extreme emergencies.

Gloria thought it would be best if they all went back to the hotel and freshened up before planning their next move. On the way back to the hotel Amelia quickly sketched the image of the hotel she had seen in Andrew's mind hoping that she could get it close enough. One of her favorite ways to cope with the stress of the job when she was alive was to sketch and paint landscapes. Once she was finished, she showed the sketch to Andrew who suggested a couple changes. After she finished them Amelia, showed Gloria and Marsha the sketch and Marsha recognized the image as the front of the Hotel Del Grande.

Marsha contacted Walter she knew that he was friends with the manager and head concierge at the hotel and could most likely find out who they were dealing with and if he was still there without alerting the mysterious vampire if he was still there. Gloria told the driver to head towards Del Grande hoping they could capture the mysterious vampire. The driver told her they about ninety minutes away.

Little over an hour later Marsha received a call from Walter telling her that the vampire travels under the alias Carlos Arturo it was believed that his real name is Taharqa he was turned in eight-ninety BC. He is wanted in Europe by lead enforcer and three possibly four different covens. He seems to have a thing for young males especially those under the protection of powerful vampires. His last known location was in Crete where he kidnapped the youngest son of the leader of largest coven in Chania. Nikos remains were found in Paris two weeks later. He was just eighteen years old. Rumors say that Taharqa has the ability to control people like puppets even vampires that had gone feral. Taharqa is known to have several large estates that he will flee to when things get too hot since he is under the protection of Rodrigues and the members of the Rios Cartel. He also told her that it was believed that he was holed up in his suite, and that he had three visitors one of them matched the description of Amsu.

They had been decided after much debate that Andrew and Amelia would make contact with the manager while Gloria and Marsha would watch the main entrance while Richard would watch the entrance to the parking garage. Once Andrew and Amelia were done with the manager Gloria and Marsha would join them on the floor to act as back up incase Amelia and Andrew had trouble-subduing Taharqa. The reason that the two of them were chosen to make entry was because of their ability to mask that they were vampires from other vampires.

Frank Arondale the hotel manager meant Andrew and Amelia in the lobby telling them that Mr. Arturo was in the penthouse suite and as far as he knew, he was alone in the room right now. The manager handed them the passkey and pleaded with them to try to be subtle as possible. The last thing that He needed was for the two of them to cause a major incident in his hotel.

Andrew and Amelia took the elevator up to the penthouse level. The two of them carefully shielded themselves against detection wanting surprise on their side. Once they arrived on the floor, they went to the entrance of the penthouse trying to make sure he was alone. As soon as Amelia got close to the door, she was able to sense overwhelming fear coming from what she was sure was a young human and by the scent, it was a male.

Immediately Andrew had an image of Jake being at the mercy of that vampire he had seen in his visions. Before Amelia could stop him, his feral side came forward and he burst through the door causing it to shatter into a million pieces. He quickly zeroed in on his target the vampire was in the process of raping the young male as he drained him of blood. Andrew hit the older vampire before he could even react driving him from the lad and into the wall as he ripped into his left side. The older vampire hadn't sensed Andrew's approach so he was caught off guard and put on the defensive.

He tried to take control of Andrew's but found it shielded he could also feel that someone else was trying to take control of his mind and he noted that Amelia was gaining the upper hand in the battle. Normally he would be able to shield his mind against her attacks but Andrew's physical attacks were taking too much of his focus and energy. Amelia's constant mental attacks were preventing him from taking control of Andrew's mind. He had already sensed that he wouldn't be able to take control of Amelia's mind without his full concentration he realized that she was just too powerful even though she was so young. Taharqa had already received several painful and deep wounds thankfully none of them were life threating he had managed to block all of the attacks that could of lead to fatal wounds. He now realized he had become over dependent on his mental abilities. It had been centuries since he had to participate in a physical altercation.

Taharqa was starting to lose his temper it seemed that he couldn't even get a decent hit in on Andrew. He couldn't believe how fast Andrew it was almost as if he was reading his mind the way he was anticipating his moves. Andrew struck again; this time he used his lengthen fingernails to rip deeply into Taharqa chest muscle. Taharqa howled in pain as he launched another flurry of blows directed at Andrew with the same result as most of his other attacks just about every one of his blows missed and the few that hit him were ineffectual at best.

Taharqa decided to change tactics if he couldn't best Andrew by a straight forward attack maybe he could use his mate against him all he had to do was get his hands on her and place her between him and Andrew then he could use her to control him. He waited until after Andrew next attack then he feigned like he was going to charge Andrew and quickly reversed direction towards Amelia. Amelia saw him coming towards her and waited until he was just about to her. She all of a sudden dropped below his grasps and as he passed over her, she stood up using her shoulder to redirect his momentum. Taharqa crashed through the ceiling tile and crashing painfully into the bottom of the concrete floor above him. His head was spinning as he fell to the floor like a sack of potatoes. As Taharqa rose, Andrew tackled him driving his nails into the left side of Taharqa chest piecing his lung.

Taharqa manage to rake his nails down the side of Andrew's face. He quickly started to slash Andrew's stomach but Andrew used his speed to move out of his range before he could damage him too badly. The two vampires circled each other trying to find an opening. Andrew feigned to the left to draw Taharqa attack and once he took the bait Andrew quickly moved to the right and drove his fingernails into Taharqa back severing the spinal cord just below the shoulders causing him to lose control of his legs. The sudden intense pain caused Taharqa to lower his mental shield and gave Amelia her chance to take control of Taharqa's mind forcing him to surrender.

Andrew quickly went to check on the boy and saw that he had already bled out. Upon looking at his identification it turned out, he was twenty-three years old and just looked young for his age. Andrew covered the man up knowing that he was in the process of being turned now. Marsha and a very pissed off Gloria came bursting through the doorway. "That was goddam foolish thing to do he could of killed you both," Gloria reprimanded angrily.

"We don't need a second mother hen I thought that was Susan's job," Andrew responded with a chuckle. He didn't see what all of the fuss was about they had handled Taharqa without too much trouble.

"Andrew one of these days the two of you are going to get yourselves in over your head you need to slow down and wait for back up. Susan and Charles will kill me if I let anything happen to the two of you." Gloria argued.

I wasn't about to stand around and wait for the two of you when that could have been Jake in there with him. The only reason he gave me any trouble was that we wanted him alive if I could have killed him he would have never even had a chance to defend himself," Andrew angrily retorted.

" I would suggest we decide what to do about the young man that is on the bed he is in the process of being turned and will need a mentor once he wakes up." Amelia said trying to defuse the argument before it went on to much farther.

"It would be simpler to prevent him from turning," Marsha said drawing a long bladed knife.

Andrew stepped between her and the unconscious's Young man. His stance showed that if Marsha wanted to get to the young man she would have to go through him. Amelia quietly stepped to Andrew's side showing her support of Andrew. "There is no way we will allow you to kill him," Andrew stated in a commanding tone.

Marsha sheathed her blade then slowly raised her hands in capitulation." Ok I will make arraignments to have him looked after." Marsha quickly said.

Marsha quickly dialed Walter's number and while she waited for him to answer she surveyed the damage to the room it wasn't as bad as she thought it would have been a few broken chairs two holes in the wall and one in the ceiling. "Walter we need a team here we have captured Taharqa but he had started the process to turn a young man and Andrew is insistent that we provide for him." Marsha quickly explained. She listened to Walter's reply before continuing, "Yes there is some minor damage to the room but Amelia and Andrew did manage to capture him alive."

While Marsha was working out the details with Walter Andrew had Amelia give him a set of the handcuffs that were designed to be used on vampires and cuffed Taharqa he then blindfolded and gagged him to prevent him from using his powers. Amelia started searching the room looking for anything that may give them a clue as to where they had taken Andrew's son.

Amelia found a bunch of papers written in a language she didn't know it sort of looked like ancient Egyptian hieroglyphics but she wasn't sure. She found Taharqa's laptop but the computer was password protected and she would time to probe Taharqa's mind in order to get the password if she could even get a pass his defenses again. Amelia knew it was Andrew's attack had caused him to lower his mental defenses and she was sure it wouldn't be as easy a second time to slip into his mind.

Twenty minutes later Walter's security team arrived and took custody of Taharqa. They had guaranteed that Andrew and Amelia would be able to interrogate him once they had him in a secured location. Just as they were about to lead him form the room when all hell broke loose

"Look out," Amelia screamed as she tackled Andrew whom was directly behind Taharqa. The window exploded then Taharqa head vaporized leaving behind a fine spray of blood mixed with brain matter all over the wall that had been in front of him. Everyone dove for cover and those that were armed pulled their weapons.

Andrew quickly checked Amelia and found her unharmed. He then crawled over to the window and peeked out looking trying to figure out where the shot had come from. He spotted two likely locations; one was a parking garage but quickly discounted it because of the angle it would have been an extremely hard shot to make.

The other was a roof of building over three hundred meters away.

Amelia had got an image of the sniper taking the shot only a brief couple of seconds before the window had exploded. She quickly realized that Andrew was in the line of fire and all of her thoughts were on saving him. Amelia was never able to reliable control this ability. She never knew how much of a warning it would give her if it gave her any at all.

The security team quickly packed up everything and with the help of Andrew, Amelia and Gloria managed to get everything into vans including the bodies before the police had arrived. Unfortunately there was no way they could clean up the crime scene which left the human authorities with a mystery to solve it was obvious that someone had been murdered in the room but the body had disappeared. The head of security had summoned the police after he found the room covered in blood. He had been called by the people staying in the adjacent room and called the front desk complaining about a possible fight in the room next to hers. She claimed hearing an argument and then to sound of glass breaking. He stated that it had taken him no more than five minutes to get to the room and upon finding, the condition it was in he did a cursory check to see if anyone needed assistance then secured the room until the police arrived.

Andrew and Amelia went to investigate the top of the building to see if his hunch was right about where the sniper had been located. He was going to go alone but Amelia wouldn't hear of it but he had managed to convince Gloria the fewer the better. Much to his displeasure the shooter had been professional enough to police up their brass in fact the only visible sign of him being there was two marks from the bipod of the rifle. Andrew placed his hand on the spot that the shooter had laid and he saw a vague image of the woman lying under a dark colored cover. He watched the woman take the shot but unfortunately, he never saw her face. He saw that she was about five foot six and was well proportioned with light brown hair. He was sure from her tan complexion she either spent a lot of time in the sun or used tanning facilities regularly. Andrew was just about to remove his hand when one final flash of insight hit him he also was her target. Andrew stood and offered his hand to Amelia. The two of them casually walked towards the door making sure to stay invisible. As they reached the door, four officers exited on to the roof with their weapons at the ready. They were almost positive that the shooter was long gone but better safe than sorry. Amelia and Andrew quickly went through the door before it closed after the last officer cleared the way. The two of them quickly exited the building and headed towards the car where Gloria awaited them. Andrew knew it would be hours before the police would finish clearing the scene and he felt bad he couldn't tell them they were wasting their time. Once they were in the car and on their way Andrew relayed what he had found out leaving out the part about him being a target.

"Andrew what are you holding back and don't you dare lie to me! I can sense that you are hiding something from me," Amelia demanded.

"Hun it is nothing important..." He started to try to lie.

"Don't you fucking hun me when you are lying. Now tell me what the fuck you are hiding or I will probe your mind and find out myself! Last fucking chance," Amelia Angrily threatened.

"Amelia it is just that I was also her target we both know that Amsu wants us dead. So nothing like I said nothing important. Don't you ever threaten to probe my mind again," Andrew retorted his anger starting to show.

"Andrew that is not nothing, that bitch had you in her sights and if it wasn't for Amelia's abilities you could have died." Gloria softly chastised.

"Andrew you ever try to lie to me again and I will kick your ass. I am your mate and if anything happened to you it would destroy me.' Amelia softly whispered. The hurt and anger that he had caused her was clearly visible.

"I am sorry love. You are right I should have never tried to hide that from you by lying. I promise I will never lie to you again." Andrew softly promised as he drew her into a tight hug.

The rest of the ride to the hotel was quiet. Walter had reserved them the penthouse at his hotel. The room had already been converted into a command center of a sort. He had two computers in the room with all of the information they had already. There were two phones their one with a direct line to Charles and the other with a direct line to him. There were a couple of pegboards; one had a map with all of Amsu known properties marked on it. Every one of the properties had around the clock surveillance. The other board had the location of two possible rogue vampire attacks. The first one was less than a mile from Shannon's home it had happened about eighteen hours ago. The second one was in the skid row part of town and had happened less than three hours ago.

"Gloria how should we go about trying to track Tony?" Andrew asked. He knew that Gloria had more experience in tracking rogue/feral vampires and her experience would prove invaluable to them now. He knew that if it wasn't already too late to save his son it soon would be.

"Andrew, I would suggest we try to confirm that the last attack was done by a rogue vampire and if it was, we start there as long as the hunting is good I don't imagine he will move on too quickly. I suspect they forced him to go feral by not feeding him so he is little more than a predatory animal and the only reason he showed any restraint at the house was because he was being controlled by Taharqa." Gloria explained.

"Is there any chance of bringing him back?" Amelia asked.

Gloria and Marsha both shook their heads. "Unfortunately once he went feral there is little we can do except put him out of his misery. Charles is hoping that we can capture him alive and use Amelia's abilities to get a lead on Jake," Gloria sadly replied.

Andrew had everyone gather around the map somehow he had been selected to be the leader. He stared at the map of the city for a few minutes. He brought forth his baser side to help him to understand how his quarry would think. He quickly realized that Tony would seek out an area that would provide him shelter close to easily accessible prey and gave him a good vantage point with several avenues of escape. That is what he would do if it were him. He looked over the map and quickly realized that the area of the last attack was not an idea area and he was sure that if Tony had carried out the attack he quickly moved on. He started to question Marsha about different areas of the city so he could try to narrow their search to two or three areas.

Amelia picked up on his line of thinking from their bound and started using the internet to get a look at the areas. After about two hours, they finally had three areas that were very promising and out of the three, the dock area was the most promising it had several abandoned buildings and a large homeless population in the area.

Gloria, Marsha, Amelia, and Andrew were just about to head out to begin their search when Marsha's cellphone rang seeing it was Walter's office number she quickly answered it.

"Marsha we just received a report of a possible rogue vampire attack in Tijuana. We may have gotten lucky a young vampire that witnessed the attack and from her description, it sounds like it may be Tony. Walter is trying to secure permission for you all to investigate the incident," Elaine quickly explained.

"What does Walter want us to do?" Marsha asked. She knew if they entered Mexico without permission, it could start a war.

"He said for you all to head that way but call before you cross the border both him and Charles are working on securing permission for you to enter. I am sending the information to your email now. Please share it with the others." Elaine said before hanging up.

"Lester get on the eight o' five heading south." Marsha said as she hung up the phone. After she made sure that Lester did as she requested she continued with her explanation, " There was a rogue attack in the Tijuana and the description form a young vampire that witnessed the attack it sounds like the rogue was Tony."

"Do we have permission to enter from Rodrigues?" Gloria asked.

"Walter and Charles are working on obtaining permission as we speak. I am to call them before we cross the border." Marsha explained. Marsha phone chimed letting her know she had an email. "This is most interesting," She exclaimed almost under her breath. Marsha looked up to see everyone staring at her.

"The victim of the attack last night was Lucia Martinez." Marsha quickly explained to answer their questioning looks. She then forwarded the email to the others so they could read all of the information.

After reading, the information Amelia used on of her pilfered FBI credentials to log into the DOJ database and see what she could find out about Lucia Martinez. It turned out she was well known to the DEA. Ms. Martinez was in charge of all of the cartel's businesses in Tijuana. The file had stated that she was believed to have carried out over twenty murders personally and ordered at least sixty more.

The file that Walter had sent them showed she was human but was known to have a vampire as body guard it wasn't sure if she was aware of his true nature or not. She also had three other guards that accompanied her everywhere which begged to ask what happened to the bodyguards. The file on the bodyguard that was a vampire showed he was an experienced and should have been more than a match for a single rogue parvulus.

About ten minutes before they arrived at the border Walter called Marsha and gave them the bad news, Rodrigues wouldn't grant permission for them to enter his territory. He claimed he would be glad to share any information that he attained about Jake. Marsha told the driver to turn around and head back to the hotel.

"You can let us out here." Andrew said catching Marsha and Gloria by surprise.

"What do you mean let you out here?" Marsha asked with a sinking feeling this was going to turn ugly.

"No, he said us my dear do you think we are going to lose our best chance of finding Andrew's son because of politics?" Amelia retorted harshly.

"Amelia, Andrew; what are you going to do?" Gloria asked hoping to find a way to reason with them.

"What do you think we are going to do? We are going to go find Tony and find out where Jake is and no one or nothing is going to stop us," Andrew replied his eyes starting to darken.

"Andrew while I sympathize with you if you cross the border you could very well start a war. That I cannot allow you to do, it is too dangerous for us all." Marsha said firmly.

"How are you planning on stopping us?" Amelia asked her eyes locked with Marsha's eyes. Amelia quickly and forcefully pushed into Marsha mind taking control. She ordered, "Tell the driver to pull over and let us out."

Marsha immediately complied but the driver refused to pull over. He kept driving and started to call Walter when Amelia took control of his mind and ordered him to pull over which he immediately did.

"What the hell do you two think you are doing?" Gloria demanded.

"What we have to do Gloria please don't make us fight you also," Andrew replied hoping not to have to fight her. He would do it and try not to hurt her but he had to get to Jake.

"Andrew trust Charles and Susan. They will find a way for you to save him without causing a war." Gloria pleaded.

"I am sorry but I can't wait for political bullshit. If Jake hasn't been turned or killed he soon will be. Tell Charles we are sorry but we have to do this." Andrew explained.

Gloria lowered her head she knew that the only way she would stop them was to incapacitate or kill them and she couldn't fight them "Please be careful. I will do what I can to help you but most likely it will be just the two of you from here on out. As soon as you can get to an ATM and draw out as much cash as you can. Here are a few numbers and addresses of places where you can obtain blood from while you are south of the border." Gloria said hoping they would be ok. She wondered how bad the fall out would be and momentarily thought about trying to stop them but she just couldn't bring herself to do it.

Both Andrew and Amelia gave her a quick hug and thanked her for all of her help. They promised to keep in touch with her and update her as often as possible. Amelia then ordered Marsha and the driver to sleep for thirty minutes and to forget that Gloria had helped them. Gloria waited until the two of them had about a ten minutes head start then called Charles. Once he answered, she quickly gave him a run down on what had happened. She finished her explanation with, "I am sorry but I couldn't stop them."

"They are away, good; please tell me they didn't hurt Walter's people?" Charles asked as if he was expecting them to do this very thing.

"They are both unharmed sleeping for the moment. Charles you are talking as if you wanted them to do this." Gloria asked suspiciously.

"Of course I knew they would do something like this I even warned Walter to expect it and we both agreed it would be best to let them do it. This way there can be no war and Andrew will still be able to do what is needed. I have already alerted our people in Mexico to keep an eye on them and assist if necessary but do not interfere." Charles finished his explanation with a small chuckle.

"Charles they think they're on their own and will take steps to make sure they can't be found." Gloria replied

" Good I am expecting them to do as much however I am sure that they will at least keep one of the cell phones and will check phone messages if they won't answer them if for no other reason than Catherine is due very soon. I will contact them soon and let them know that we are still supporting them," Charles said.

The first thing Amelia and Andrew did after they left the van was to find an ATM machine and get as much cash as they could. Next, they went and brought vehicle. They settled on an older GMC Jimmy it looked a little worn but it ran great. The owner of the lot was surprised when the two of them said they would pay cash for it.

The two of them were surprised that Charles, Susan or Walter had not tried to call them. They had already agreed to talk to Charles or Susan because they were valued friends. They both hoped that their friendship wouldn't end because of this but if that were the price, they would have to pay it. As they headed towards the border, the two of them knew that they were on their own for here on out.

Andrew and Amelia had little trouble getting through customs. They had claimed that they were going site seeing for a few days and thanks to a little push from Amelia the guard wouldn't recall even meeting them. Andrew pulled into the first gas station they came to. While he was filling the truck up Amelia went into the small store and got them a map and a newspaper. The murder of Lucia Martinez was still in the headlines as was two other attacks. Amelia wondered if Charles knew of these other attacks yet. She also grabbed a couple bottles of water and a large bag of chips. She then paid for her stuff and headed back across the lot. She knew that she was being watched and casually glanced around to see if she could spot from where when Andrew voice came into her mind, "Yes love we are being followed. It's the two vampires in that dark blue Fusion about forty meters to your right. They have been with us since we left the border."

"Do you think they work for Rodrigues or are they police?" Amelia asked mentally

"That is a good question. I am planning on leading them to a secluded area and finding out; are you game?" Andrew replied the same way.

Amelia smiled and gave him a subtle nod as she got into the Jimmy. Andrew quickly joined her and the two of them headed towards the area where Lucia Martinez was murdered. Andrew was hoping that he could get some kind of a lead to where Tony was by using his ability to read objects. He knew that would have to lose their tail before he could make the attempt. Andrew started to meander around the streets as if he was not sure where he was going in an attempt to find a location to confront their pursuers. Andrew noticed an alleyway that didn't have anybody in it when an idea hit him and he decided to go with it. Andrew quickly turned into it he accelerated to get ahead of the car that was following him and at the end of the alley hung a quick right. He heard the wheels squeal as the truck protested the change in direction. Andrew quickly accelerated using every bit of horsepower the eight cylinders could produce as he weaved through the traffic at the next corner he made a left turn cutting across three lanes of traffic the ass end of the truck violently fishtailed as Andrew fought for control. Once the truck had settled down and quickly accelerated trying to put as much distance between them and their tail. Andrew made a few two more quick turns; after he checked and saw that he had indeed lost the tail he resumed a more sedate driving style.

"Would you please warn me the next time you are going to pull a stunt like that? I thought we were going to question them." Amelia ground out as she pointed to the wet spot spreading across the front of her shirt.

"Sorry it was a split second decision. After thinking about it I decided it might be better to lose them instead of confronting them." Andrew replied as he shrugged his shoulders and laughed while he watched her wipe the excess water off of her shirt. He could clearly see her braless breast through the wet material. "I don't think I will warn you however, I like the results." Andrew teased as he pointed to her easily seen breast.

Amelia just rolled her eyes at him but couldn't help but chuckle. She carefully shielded her mind so he wouldn't pick up on what she was about to do. She turned herself invisible to everyone but Andrew and quickly removed her shirt. "I guess I will have to let this dry before I put it back on." She purred seductively as she started massaging her breast while pinching her nipples.

Andrew had turned his attention back to the road because traffic had picked up a little bit and glanced over to see what she was talking about. He was so surprised to see Amelia teasing her glorious breast that he almost rear-ended another car when traffic stopped short. Amelia couldn't help but Chuckle at his reaction then she slowly unbuttoned and lowered her jeans giving him an eyeful of her charms. She sensually rubbed her hand over her own mounds as she did she dipped her finger into her hot pussy then slowly brought her finger to her mouth and started to swirl her tongue around it licking her nectar off of it. She finished the licking of her finger by sticking the finger in her mouth and sucking off any remaining juices. She repeated the process several each time she gave a loud slow moan.

"Andrew darling can you think of something else I could use my hot mouth and tongue on." Amelia softly teased.

Andrew almost blew his load while just watching her and now her teasing him directly was almost more than he could stand. He quickly closed his eyes for a moment to get himself back under control. As he opened his eyes, he felt Amelia unzipped his pants and pulled his rock hard cock out. Before he could stop her, not that he was going to, she had taken his full length into her mouth and was massaging him with her throat muscles. She would intermittently raise her head until only the tip of his dick was in her mouth then she would swirl her tongue around the head of his cock before going back down until her nose was buried into his pubic hair. She took great pleasure in torturing him in this manner for a while. She then started to bob her head up and down while varying her suction and speed. She had one hand playing with her clit and used her other hand to start massaging his balls. Andrew tried to hold out against the sensations and the vision of her not only sucking his cock but also playing with herself proved too much and he roared as his balls tightened and he fired rope after rope of hot cum down his mate's throat, which Amelia greedily swallowed. She kept going until his cock softened. She then put his soft well-used member away and smiled at him. "I figured you needed that so you could relax a little." Amelia softly said with a smile. She quickly redressed after cleaning herself up.

CHAPTER 3

***

Andrew came back to his senses and wondered how he managed to drive without wrecking. He quickly looked around to get his bearing and realized that he had passed his destination several miles back. He shook his head amused at his mates' antics but she was right he felt a lot calmer now. "Thank you, you were right I do feel a lot better." He said with a smile. He wrapped his arm around her and gave her a quick kiss, "I will repay you one hundred fold when we get to the hotel." Andrew promised with a wicked smile.

"Hun we are going to need to hit a store you do realize the only clothes we have are on our backs and we have none of our toiletries." Amelia reminded him.

"Not to mention we are going to need blood the day after tomorrow the latest." Andrew added as he made a U- turn and headed back towards their original destination.

While Andrew was driving, she quickly called the first number on the list Gloria had given her and was surprised to find out this place wasn't one of Susan's subsidiaries. The vampire that had answered the call wanted to know if they wanted a live donor or bagged blood. He stated that he would deliver the product anywhere within Mexico within eight hours the price was forty-five thousand Pecos or thirty-five hundred American dollars for bagged blood guaranteed fresh from live donors. If they wanted a live donor, it would be three point two million Pecos or a quarter of a million dollars American that included disposal of the body once they were done. Amelia told him she would call back once they had gotten a hotel room.

They were a couple of blocks from where Lucia Martinez had been murdered when Andrew sensed the vampires that had been tailing them. He pulled over far enough back so that the other vampires wouldn't sense them. Amelia glanced over at Andrew curious why he had pulled over all suddenly. "Our friends from earlier are down the street. I want to watch them for a while and if they leave we will follow them." Andrew explained.

"Ok that makes sense but what if they are waiting for us?" Amelia asked as she shielded herself so the other vampires couldn't detect her. Both Andrew and she were surprised when Gloria mentioned that they had the ability to hide the fact that are vampires from other of their species. Normally a vampire can detect another of its kind just from being in the same area as another vampire. Gloria had discovered this about them when they had captured Uwais.

Amelia and Andrew set there for several hours watching the vampires in the other vehicle and realized that the other vampires intended to stay until they spotted the two of them. Both Andrew and Amelia suggested at the same time that it was time to approach the other vampires to find out whom they were working for, and what were their intentions were. After a small laugh, they both talked over several plans before deciding that Amelia would approach the car driving the truck, which she would use to block the driver's side doors. She would then try to take control of the driver while Andrew would shield himself from detection, approach the passenger side, and subdue the other vampire. They would attempt to take both of them alive so they could have a pleasant little chat with them.

Andrew stepped out of the vehicle and turned invisible to everyone except Amelia. He also made sure that they wouldn't be able to sense him and cautiously moved towards the car. Once he got in position, he mentally told Amelia he was ready. She drove the truck down the street slowly as if looking for an address not wanting to alert the vampires in the Fusion as she pulled alongside she quickly turned the wheel of the truck and used the front bumper to block the driver doors effectively trapping the driver in the car. Amelia quickly exited the Jimmy and moved to where she could see the drivers eyes and after a brief mental struggle; she easily took control of his mind and ordered him not to move.

The other vampire seeing his partner in trouble quickly exited the fusion and was immediately grabbed by the throat and slammed against the side of the car as Andrew came visible. Moving at inhuman speed he quickly disarmed the vampire and placed the vampires own gun under his chin. "Give me one good reason why I Shouldn't kill you right now?" Andrew demanded as he pressed the barrel a little harder into the vampires throat.

Armin eyes went wide in shock when he felt himself being snatched by the throat and slammed against the car he had just exited. He couldn't figure out how he had missed the parvulus. He hadn't sensed another vampire around him. "Andrew, we work for Charles Black and have a message for you." The vampire quickly replied after getting over his initial shock.

Andrew glanced over at Amelia and she nodded slightly indicating that the vampire was telling the truth she had managed to confirm the information from Edward the vampire she had under her control. Andrew lowered the gun from under Armin's chin much to Armin's relief. "Dam Charles said you two were some of the best he had seen but I thought he was exaggerating. I am Armin Santiago at your service. Edward Gerardo the vampire that is under your lovely mates control is my partner.

Charles asked us to make contact with you. Here is a list of safe houses where you can go if you get into trouble they will provide you with shelter and aid. We also have a cooler with a few days' supply of blood and twenty units of plasma. I also have a laptop and a secure cell phone for you. The phone is programed with numbers of contacts that may be able to help you. Eddy has a letter from Charles that will explain everything but we really need to go someplace more private to discuss these matters." Armin explained in a low tone.

Amelia backed the truck away from the door of the Fusion and parked it. She looked to make sure she hadn't caused any damage to the car which had not she then released Edward from her control after she told him to remain where he was and not to move until she said to. After hearing Armin explanation she asked, "Edward may I have the letter for Andrew and I?"

Edward slowly reached into his jacket pocket and handed the envelope containing the papers that Charles had faxed to them to give to Amelia or Andrew. Amelia quickly read the letter from Charles. "Love The letter is form Charles and he asked us to trust him. They are here to assist us. "Amelia said using telepathy.

Andrew released Armin and handed him back his weapon. "Sorry about the mistake but we can't be too careful. I hope you understand."

"No harm done I would have done the same thing if I were in your shoes. Will you please follow me to a place where we can talk?" Armin asked as he holstered his gun.

"We will follow you or we can meet you if you think it would be better." Andrew offered in response.

Armin gave Andrew the address of the warehouse they were going to incase the two vehicles got separated. Andrew had no trouble following the other car and within twenty minutes, they had arrived at their destination. Both Andrew and Amelia were impressed with the operation here inside of the warehouse were four large tractor and trailers and about a half of dozen tables covered in maps each of the trailers was loaded with sophisticated equipment to monitor all forms of communication. They also had racks of television screens each one tuned to a different local channel located somewhere in Mexico or Central America. As Amelia scanned the information on some of the small monitors, she quickly realized that if the US government ever got a hold of the information here they would be able to wipe out the drug trade in a few days.

Armin gave them a quick tour of the operation explaining it was one of four, which Charles had scattered around Mexico. He brought them up to date on the current situation between Charles and Rodrigues. He warned them that once Rodrigues found out that the two of them were in his territory he would have them hunted down as rogues. He then offered to drive them back to the place where the other two of Martinez's people had been killed. Armin and Edward both warned them to stay away from the area that Lucia Martinez had been killed.

Armin took Amelia and Andrew to the locations that the other murders unfortunately the area had had too many others for Andrew psychometry to work. After they visited both of the locations, Armin took them to a nice little diner for an early breakfast. He gave them information on the local culture and going one. He also more importantly suggested areas they should try to avoid. Armin also told them that he would monitor the local police bands and let the two of them know if there was any suspicious murder that way hopefully the two of them could get to the scene while it was still fresh. After they had returned to the warehouse, Edward showed them an area where they could rest for a few hours.

While Armin and Edward tended to Andrew and Amelia, a group of vampires was reading their Jimmy they added a large cooler with twenty units of blood that could be plugged into a cigarette lighter. They also added additional power outlets and a power converter that way they could use the truck to charge the laptop or their cell phone. The inverter that was installed actually had enough power to run a small appliance. They also installed a navigation system and went over the truck to make sure it was mechanically sound. They added a couple suitcases of clothes in Amelia and Andrew sizes. Hidden in the bottom of each suitcase were a Glock twenty-one with a couple clips and a Kukri.

Armin woke Amelia and Andrew at a little after ten Am and said that they had a phone call from Charles. The two of them quickly rose from the cots they were sleeping on and as they followed Armin to where the phone was a young vampire named Leticia handed them each a cup of very strong coffee. It turned out that Leticia was Edwards mate and as they found out few hours later one hell of a cook. Armin led them to one of the trailers and handed Andrew the phone.

"Good morning Charles," Andrew said as he waited to hear the lecture he was expecting.

"Good morning Andrew I hope you and Amelia had a good rest," Charles replied. After Andrew confirmed they had; he continued, "Andrew I hope that you understand I cannot help you openly without starting a war. Please be on your guard at all times and don't trust anyone except for Armin, Edward and Edwards mate Leticia. In the computer, that they have for you is everything that both Walter's and my organizations know about Rodrigues and his organization. Before you leave the warehouse Armin will make sure, you have a list of safe houses for you to go to if necessary. Gloria will continue with the investigation in California. Andrew if Rodrigues captures you he won't hesitate to kill both you and Amelia so please be extra careful. Susan will make my life a living hell if anything happens to either of you."

The two of them talked for a bit more before hanging up .Charles said to tell Amelia that Catherine was doing good and he would contact them as soon she had the baby. Just before he hung up, he told Andrew to have Edward give you a satellite phone there are a lot of areas where a regular phone won't get reception. Charles had Edward give him a beeper and made sure he got the number. He stated half-jokingly that they would work in areas that even a sat-phone won't.

Gloria and Richard were asked to locate Harry he hadn't been seen since the night that Shannon had been murdered. Walter had tried to reach him by phone but his cell had to be turned off since it went straight to voicemail. Richard was driving the two of them to Harry's home; it seemed to most logical place to start their search for him. The house was located in an upper middle-class suburban area just outside of the city. It was a four-bedroom rancher with the proverbial white picket fence around it. They both noticed that Harry's fifty-eight T-Bird was in the driveway. The two of them knocked on the door a few times with no answer then

Gloria looked around to make sure that no one was watching the two of them then she quickly picked the lock on the front door. Cautiously she opened the door and stepped in going to the right while Richard went to the left. Gloria found the reason why no one had heard from Harry and his mate they were both on the bed while their heads were on their respective nightstands. Richard quickly called Walter had had a cleanup team dispatched. While they waited for the team, the two of them started to go through the house looking for clues as to who had done this.

Amelia and Andrew left the warehouse and headed towards Martinez's territory hoping to pick up Tony's trail. They found a small hotel near the center of their area and checked in, they knew they were taking a chance attracting attention of the local cartel but decided the risk was worth it. Andrew was taking a shower while Amelia was going over what information they had on the suspected rogue attacks and she was beginning to suspect that they weren't as random as they seemed to be. It looked as if someone was using rogues to cover up planned attacks that were designed to weaken the Martinez cartel and it had been going on for almost a year. If Amelia was correct, no fewer than eight key members had been eliminated by being attacked by rogue vampires in the last four months. The deaths were covered up allegedly to hide the existence of vampires.

Amelia broadened the search to the Perez cartel it was the first cartel that the Rios cartel had taken over after Rodrigues had assumed control. The results from the local news reports were enlightening; Several of Perez's top lieutenants were killed under mysterious circumstances, four of them the original cause of death was unexplained exsanguination. According to the one article, Carlos Perez's body had been almost completely drained of blood and the medical examiner stated that there were no injuries serious enough to have caused such a massive loss of blood.

She continued to the article on the next victim Anglia Santiago had been drained of blood while in police custody. She had been one of Carlos Perez's mistresses and witnessed his death. She had given a wild story about a man who had bite Carlos on the neck and drank his blood. She claimed she hide and watched the events unfold. Whoever had killed had managed to do it while she was locked in a cell. In order to get to the cell you had to use a designated elevator that required a key then go through locked door with a guard seated right in front of it. There were also eight other officers in the building. The person who perpetrated this crime managed to get past all of this without being seen by any of the six different cameras and not one of the officers in the building seeing them.

Amelia looked up from the computer and saw Andrew was seated on the edge of the bed waiting for her. She had been sharing everything she had learned through their link without even realizing it. The small smile he had on his face all of sudden changed to a scowl while his eyes started to darken and he turned towards the door. Amelia quickly brought forth her baser self as she now sensed what had set Andrew off. The two of them could sense another vampire and they both knew that the other vampire was much older than two of them were. Amelia quickly reached into the suitcase beside her and tossed Andrew the kukri that was in it afterwards she grabbed the Glock and chambered the first round.

"Love get in the bathroom that way you will have a clear line of fire at the door and window while still having some cover." Andrew telepathically said as he moved to the side of the door.

Amelia quickly moved to where Andrew had asked her to, she then turned invisible to everyone but Andrew and shielded her presence in order to give her a better chance. She noted that Andrew had also shielded his presence. Next came the hard part waiting to see what the other vampire was going to do. After a few minutes, much to their surprise came; a knock at the door and an announcement that the other vampire just wanted to talk. "Please stay as you are while I answer the door. If this is an ambush you can cover me without exposing yourself." Andrew pleaded using telepathy.

Although Amelia was clearly not happy, she agreed to Andrew's plan. Andrew reigned in his baser side while he slide the Kukri in between his belt and Pants making sure it was where he quickly could retrieve it. He could sense the vampire at the door and three more down the end of the hall. He mentally prepared himself incase this was an ambush and opened the door trying to appear as calm as possible. Once he had the door open he saw an older Hispanic man that stood almost six- feet tall and weighed about hundred and seventy pounds. Even though he looked about sixty Andrew knew that he was much older. Andrew stepped back and invited him into the room.

"Thank you for receiving me. I was told that your mate was here but I guess my information was wrong. I am Santiago Martinez." The vampire said as way of introduction.

"Greetings Mr. Martinez, I am Andrew Barnes and that is my lovely mate Amelia." Andrew replied, as Amelia turned visible after reigning in her baser side.

Even though Amelia had surprised him, Santiago Martinez hide it well. His face only showed his shock for the briefest of a moment before he regained control and offered a slight Smile. "Ms. Hensley reports on how lovely you are were greatly lacking." Martinez said as he took her offered hand and kissed it.

Amelia smiled at the charming older vampire and while she sensed apprehension, she didn't sense any hostility. She could understand his concern when he found out he had two new vampires in his territory with all of the attacks against his people. "Please have a seat." Amelia offered with a cautious smile.

He took the offered seat and Study his two hosts. He sensed that while they were both wary of him they held no real hostility towards him or his family if anything he sensed a bit of amusement from Amelia. He knew the two of them were somehow associated with Charles Black and last he had heard they were under Black's personal protection. That is why He had decided to meet with the two of them personally. "I apologize for the intrusion but I am curious as to why two of Black's people are here in my territory and what your intentions are?" Santiago asked deciding to lay his cards on the table.

"We are here looking for a link that could lead me to the location of my human son. I assume you have heard about the attack in California," Andrew replied deciding it would be better to tell him the truth. He held back the part that the link was a rogue vampire that may be attacking his family.

"Then you aren't tracking the rogue vampire that was turned when your wife was murdered?" Santiago asked already knowing the answer. He was impressed how both of them had managed to hid their surprise Amelia had only showed the slightest of reaction to his statement and Andrew had shown none.

"We are seeking the rogue we are hoping to capture him to try to garner the location of my mate's son before we destroy him." Amelia responded she saw no sense in trying to cover it up now that it was evident he knew more than he should of.

"Then it would seem that it would be in my best interest to allow the two of you go about your business. I have one final question is Rodrigues behind these attacks on my family?" Santiago inquired his eyes darkening.

Andrew hesitated for a moment deciding how much to share with Santiago. He glanced at Amelia for a moment, she gave the slightest of nod knowing what he was planning on saying, and agreeing it was best to be honest.

"We suspect that he is somehow controlling the rogues but have no real proof at this point. I promise you if we find out he is carrying out these attacks I will make sure you receive the proof we gather and will also do my best to convince Charles to act accordingly." Andrew promised. He thought to himself how funny this situation was a year ago he and Amelia would have been trying to arrest this very man and no he promising to aid him.

"Thank you, I appreciate the offer. One final warning for you Rodrigues knows you are in the area if he finds you he will either kill you outright or you wish he had if he does capture you." Santiago said.

Neither Amelia nor Andrew fully trusted Santiago. They both knew the only reason he was tolerating their presence in his territory was he was hoping they would take care of the rogue problem for him and his kindly grandfather persona was just a ruse to try to fish for information. The two of them discussed the offer Andrew had made to share information and decided to honor it as long as it didn't compromise any of Charles or Susan's interest.

The next week was quiet no mysterious attacks had happened on either side of the border adding to the credence that these weren't true rogue attacks. The two of them had talked to Charles twice keeping him informed of what they had managed to find out. The three of them had set up a schedule where Andrew or Amelia would make contact with Charles. They decided to vary the days and times and they decided that if Charles needed to contact them he would send them an e-mail with a contact time unless it was important then he would page them.

Amelia had called Catherine on Friday and talked to her for over an hour. Catherine had assured her that she was doing great, as was the baby and promised her that Scott would page them as soon as she went into labor. Amelia had been feeling a little down about not being with her and talking to Catherine had helped her.

A week after Amelia had talked to Catherine, Amelia and Andrew decided to go to a small café for dinner. They had just ordered when Andrew received a page informing them that Catherine water had broken and she was in labor. After the two of them finished their meal, Amelia called to check on how Catherine was doing. She talked to Susan who reassured her that everything was going excellent and she promised to text Amelia with all of the details. Several hours later, they received a text that read.

Brittney Lynn Hawkins was born at one-sixteen AM, She weighed seven pounds eleven and one –half ounces and was seventeen inches long. Mom and daughter are doing well, dad on other hand not doing so well. I will email you a picture soon, Susan.

Amelia and Andrew anxiously waited for the picture and as soon as they saw the picture, they fell instantly in love with her. She was fully awake when the picture was taken shaken her little fist at the world. Amelia was surprised to find out that Brittney had a full head of brown hair and piercing blue eyes. Andrew quickly made her picture the background picture on their laptop.

The next evening they caught a break. Gloria had as a normal part of her investigation had flagged Tony's bank and credit cards so they would get an alert if they were used. The card had been used in a nightclub called El Pozo Del Diablo (The Devil's Pit) to make a large purchase. The nightclub was located in the business district of Tijuana. She immediately sent the information to Amelia and Andrew.

Amelia was beginning to think that either Tony had been caught and killed or had moved on and she was explaining to Andrew why she thought that they should start looking towards Mexico city since that was where Rodrigues was based. If he were working with Amsu then it would be the next logical place to look for Jake. Andrew did agree with Amelia but wanted to give it a few more days before they moved. Amelia was just about to point out that that the longer they stayed here the more likely that Jake would be turned or killed when the pager went off.

The location that Gloria had given them was about twenty minutes away. The club was an old textile plant that had closed in the late sixties. Carlos Guerrero purchased the building and converted it to a large nightclub that catered to vampires. The two of them arrived within ten minutes taking the first available parking place. Amelia had just stepped out of the truck when a little girl walked up to her. "Are you Senorita Barnes?" The child asked nervously.

"Yes I am." Amelia responded cautiously. She was suspicious and quickly went on alert. Andrew heard the girl and quickly went on alert pushing his senses out. He couldn't detect any threat to them so he but stayed alert to allow Amelia to deal with the child.

"I was told to give you this message when you arrived." The little girl said handing Amelia an envelope.

"Thank you sweetie." Amelia said while handing her a twenty-dollar bill. Amelia had scanned her mind and found out she was just what she appeared to be a child that had been giving a few pesos to give her the message.

When the young girl saw s twenty American Dollars she almost fainted. "Muchas gracias, vaya con dios." The young girl called out excitedly as she ran down the street towards home.

Amelia quickly opened the envelope and read the message.

Amelia and Andrew,

I am the one who used Tony's credit card because I need to meet with you. I give you my word of honor and swear to all I hold holly that this is no trap. Please hear what I have to say it may mean the survival of every one of us. Please go to the door and tell the bouncer you are meeting with Layla. Please hurry we are all in danger

Amsu and Rodrigues Know you are here in Tijuana and are looking for you. I will even help you to find your son if I can.

Amelia read the letter twice both times mentally relaying the contents to Andrew. The two of them were in shock and unsure what to do. Andrew grabbed his phone and dialed Charles number. As soon as Charles answered, he relayed the contents of the letter then he asked, "Is Layla trust worthy?"

"Under normal circumstances I would say that you could trust her. However, I would caution you to be extraordinary careful when dealing with anyone related to Amsu. If you decide to meet with her don't let your guard down even if she is being honest Amsu won't take her defection lightly." Charles replied his voice thick with concern.

They decided that Andrew would be invisible this time and Amelia would approach her if everything was copasetic he would come visible and get the three of them to a safe location. If it turned out to be a trap, Andrew would then cause a diversion so that the two of them would be able to escape. Amelia approached the bouncer who was manning the front door of the club and told him she was with Layla's party. The vampire looked her over for a moment then opened the door allowing her to enter telling her that the room was on the second floor to the left. Amelia paused in front of the bouncer smiled and gave him her thanks allowing Andrew to slip through the door. Amelia led the two of them up the stairs and down the short hall to the door. Andrew reached out with his senses to see if he could sense in the room. He sensed only one vampire that seemed to be pacing.

Amelia quickly entered the private room followed closely by Andrew. Amelia cautiously looked around the room making sure there was no one else there other than Layla, Andrew, and herself. "Ok Layla you asked for this meeting; now what is on your mind?" Amelia demanded in a cold voice.

"Amelia I am not your enemy. I need yours and Andrew's help to prevent this war that Amsu wants he will kill us all." Layla pleaded earnestly. She sensed when Amelia started to probe her and she allowed it not offering any resistance. Layla had heard that Amelia had the ability to read other people's minds and knew this was her best chance to secure their assistance.

Amelia was aware that Layla was able to tell that she was reading her thoughts and was surprised when Layla hadn't resisted her probing her mind. Amelia quickly realized that Layla was telling the truth about her intentions and quickly withdrew from her mind satisfied that she was no threat. "Andrew she is on our side. She is telling the truth about her willingness to help us." Amelia mentally said.

"Amelia is Andrew going to join us we don't have much time," Layla asked impatiently.

"Andrew is already here," Andrew replied appearing behind her. Layla who was startled had to quickly, stifle her scream.

"I promise to tell you everything but we need to get out of here before Martinez finds out I am meeting with you or he will kill us all." Layla quickly explained.

"Martinez knows we are here and had granted us safe passage so you are safe." Amelia replied not concerned.

"Martinez is in bed with Amsu and Rodrigues. The so-called murders of his family were all executed with his knowledge and blessings. Even the one that happened in Philadelphia according to Santiago, Carlos and his two guards were getting troublesome and needed to be disposed of," Layla quickly explained.

"Are you telling us that he had his own grandson killed?" Amelia asked in shock.

"Yes. Can we please get out of here?" Layla pleaded.

Andrew sensed six vampires standing outside of the door. He was almost positive that one of them was Santiago Martinez. He didn't think they knew he was in the room because he was still shieling his presence. "Love, Martinez and five other vampires are outside of the door. I don't think they know that I am here he may suspect. I want you to try to find out his intentions and if necessary, I will capture him and use him to bargain our way out of here. If that fails I want you to get Layla clear and I will delay them long enough for you to get to the truck." Andrew said mentally.

"Hell no we will leave together. We stand together always remember." Amelia argued back telepathically.

"I have no intentions of getting myself killed but we need Layla alive now more than ever. She is the key to us stopping this war that Amsu wants before it ever starts." Andrew calmly replied the same way.

Amelia relayed the plan to Layla just to make sure that the vampires outside of the room didn't pick up on Andrew voice. She had Layla turn invisible. There was a sharp wrap at the door. "Amelia, I know you are in there with Layla. All I want is her then you can leave as can Andrew," Martinez ordered through the door.

"Mr. Martinez, Layla is under my protection. She is willing to help us not only retrieve Andrew's son but also to stop the attacks on your family," Amelia replied.

"Amelia, she can't be trusted let me have her and I promise you that I will get the location of your mates child. Is Andrew there let me talk to him?" Martinez replied in a solemn tone.

"I have promised her my protection I can't give her to you. Andrew isn't with me." Amelia lied smoothly.

"Amelia either you turn her over to me or I will take her by force. Please don't make me do that you could be killed." Martinez pleaded acting as if he was concerned for her safety.

"Mr. Martinez, are you threating me? I was trying to reason with you but since you have reverted to threats I will just give you a warning if anyone of your people tries to enter this room I will kill them." Amelia angrily threatened as she called forth her baser side.

"Amelia either surrender her or I will just toss a Molotov cocktail in there and burn you out." Martinez threatened.

Andrew had let his baser side come forth and upon hearing Martinez's threat, he just exploded. He rushed the door taking it off of the hinges and sent it flying into Martinez and the man that stood on each side of him knocking all three of them off of their feet. The man to the right of Martinez had the unfortunate luck of being struck by a large piece of the doorjamb; an eighteen-inch piece of it was now imbedded into side of his chest. He quickly turned to the vampire to his left and ripped his head off of his shoulders before any of them had a chance to react. Amelia quickly seized control of the vampire to Andrew's right and had him attack the other vampire standing beside him.

As the vampire, that Andrew had decapitated fell to the ground Andrew turned and charged Martinez. He knew the key to winning this battled was to get control of their leader and use him to shield Amelia, Layla and himself. Andrew managed to get to Martinez before he could get back on his feet and he quickly attacked him trying to subdue Martinez. Martinez was nowhere as fast as Andrew was but he had years of experience fighting other vampires that were faster them him. Andrew launched a serious of rapid blows hoping to daze Martinez long enough for him to get control of him but Martinez managed to block or dodge all but one of them and the that he had landed was not as effective as he had hoped. Martinez countered with a knee to Andrew's groin but he managed to turn with the blow and his thigh absorbed the blow. The fight between the two of them was turning into who could a slugfest that Andrew knew he didn't have the time for. "Amelia can you please take control of this cocksucker's mind before his reinforcements get here." Andrew requested through their bond.

Layla was at first caught off guard by Andrew sudden and violent attack. She hadn't even seen him move until the door exploded off of the hinges. She had never seen a vampire move as fast as Andrew did and was in awe of his strength but she quickly recovered. Martinez was right her abilities weren't offensive in nature but that didn't mean she was useless in a fight. Amsu had made sure she was well trained with and without weapons. She held black belts in several forms of Martial arts including Wing Chu, Aikido, Kyudo, and her favorite Yijin Jing.

She quickly attacked the other vampire that was on the left hand side. She had the vampire's head in her hands after a couple minutes. The poor lad was too young and inexperienced to be much of a threat.

Amelia was still trying to get into position where she could see Martinez's eyes while Andrew was fighting with him the other vampire that Andrew had knocked to the ground was now under Amelia's control he was helping the first vampire that Amelia had taken control of.

Martinez was impressed that Andrew was doing so well but he was also boring of the fight. It had been entertaining but now he wanted it over. He delivered a hard kick to Andrew's stomach followed by a quick uppercut to his jaw. Martinez then used his talon like finger nails to rip open Andrew's chest. Martinez was about to punch into the opened chest and remove Andrew's heart when out of desperation Andrew used his telekinesis to slam him into the ceiling and then let him drop to the ground. Martinez hadn't known that Andrew had telekinetic abilities and now he was paying the price for that lack of information he had tried to use his mind control abilities on him but his mind was shielded unbeknownst to him by Amelia. Every time she felt Martinez push into Andrew mind to take control, she would reinforce Andrew's mental defenses.

Andrew used his telekinesis to slam Martinez head first into the wall, stunning him and giving Amelia the chance she needed to take control of Martinez's mind and after a brief but hard fought mental struggled, she had managed to gain control of him and ordered him to surrender. Andrew was grateful he needed some time to heal and regain his strength.

Amelia ordered Martinez to order his men to stand down. After he had done that she ordered one of the other two men she had control of to get there vehicle and move up by the rear entrance. Just as they were getting ready to move about a dozen of Martinez men came pouring through the door all of them heavily armed much to Andrew and Amelia's relief only three of them were vampires. Amelia made Martinez order them to stand down but the three vampires knowing that Martinez was under Amelia's control was reluctant to comply with his orders. The largest of the vampires stepped forward blocking the hall. "You will release Mr. Martinez and turn the woman over to us or you will die." He ordered.

Andrew quickly placed himself between the large vampire and his mate. Effectively he blocked the vampire's path to Amelia and the others. "Move out our way this instant," Andrew ordered.

The large vampire withdrew his O'Tanto, "Parvulus I would suggest that you not tempt fate if I am forced to attack your mate will suffer the consequences. I will admit it will be fun making her pay." The large vampire threatened with a snide look on his face.

Andrew's eyes darkened as his baser side took control. "Do you want to see consequences cocksucker?" Andrew asked in a deadly ice laced voice that was just above a whisper.

Andrew's eyes darkened even more and the vampire in front of him began to scream in agony. The blade of the sword he had been brandishing turned to molten steel and ran down his hand. All watched in horror as smoke started to pour out of the large vampire's mouth and nose just before his body erupted in flames. The two other vampires who had been standing with him turned to run but before they could make a single step, the two of them disappeared in a maelstrom of flames and smoke. Layla eyes opened wide in shock as she watched the events unfold not sure what to do. She had heard rumors that Andrew had killed some street thug by using pyrokinesis but didn't believe he possessed such powers at such a young age.

The humans that had been with the vampires just dropped their weapons and ran as fast as they could. They had seen a lot of weird shit since they had started working for Martinez Cartel but this was too much. Just as the nine of them reached the bottom of the stairs, the sprinkler system went off followed closely by the screaming of the fire alarm causing a general panic in the club with everyone racing for the exits. People were being trampled in the mad rush.

Amelia was concerned that Andrew was losing himself once more to his baser side but was surprised when as soon as the threat had been neutralized his baser side had retreated and Andrew seemed to return to normal. She kept a close eye on her mate as he lead down the steps and through the crowd towards the rear exit. They had placed Layla between the two of them and had Martinez and his goon flanking her to act as a shield. Just as they reached the rear exit Andrew sensed Amsu. "Dammit! Amsu is heading towards us." Andrew was not sure how he knew the vampires heading towards him without seeing them but he knew he was right. Andrew opened the door after everyone else was starting to get into their truck .Andrew wanted to delay Amsu. He could sense that the club was empty of almost everyone but those that were with Amsu so he felt it was safe to take a risk. He formed an image of the floor of the building being a large campfire when all of suddenly the floor in front of him erupted into flames and rapidly spread as if the entire floor had been doused in gas. He watched as Amsu and his men raced for the door. Andrew heard the death screams of several vampires as he turned and quickly got into the truck with the rest

Amelia ordered the driver to head towards the northwestern end of town.

Once the vehicle was under way Amelia decided to attempt to scan Martinez's mind hoping he knew where Jake was and if Layla was telling the truth. She found out that he was in bed with Amsu. In fact, Martinez had planned the murder of Andre's ex-wife. Amsu was going to use the murder to prove that Charles had become a weak and ineffectual leader after all he couldn't even protect a human woman. She saw that Amsu had made a three-way alliance between Martinez, Rodrigues and himself. After the war, he promised that Rodrigues would be head enforcer for all of the America's and Martinez would get Europe including the former USSR. Amsu original plan included Charles but after diamond had been killed, he blamed him for not helping him to save her. The last item she pulled from Martinez's mind was the location of Jake he was being held at one of Martinez's villas in Mexico City. Amelia quickly relayed what she had pried out of Martinez's mind to Andrew and Layla.

"How long would it take us to fly to there?" Andrew asked.

"Too long Amsu would already have him moved. He has three other villas he can move him to in that city and twenty more within an hour's drive," Layla replied. She paused for a few minutes trying to decide how much she should divulged to them. She cautiously studied Andrew's face she was sure he was the one who was in charge. "Andrew two things you need to know first of all he can track me since he is my sire. Secondly, he has turned your son more to the point he had me turn Jake. I am sorry but it was either I turned him or Amsu was going to kill him." Layla continued hoping that Andrew wouldn't kill her.

Andrew stomped on the brake pedal so hard that he actually bent it his eyes darkened and his fangs came out. "You did what?" He asked his voice cold as the grave.

"Andrew if I didn't he would be dead. Amsu was going to rip out his throat and I convinced him that it would be more advantageous to turn him. I'm so sorry but I didn't know what else to do and I could let that precious child die. I even managed to convince Amsu that he would be a good addition to his organization once he got a little more experience," Layla explained quickly wondering if she would live another five minutes.

"Love she is telling the truth she was trying to protect Jake. I managed to read that much from her when she was telling you what happened. She is extremely protective of him. I even read that she was able to keep him from seeing his mother murdered," Amelia quickly told him through their bond.

Andrew took a couple quick deep breathes to calm himself down once he was back in control of himself he started to drive again. "Layla thank you for what you have done for Jake. Correct me if I am wrong but because you are his sire you can track him," He asked praying he was right.

"I can track him unless he is shielding himself. I am hoping that Amsu won't be able to override my compulsion. I ordered him to never shield himself from me but we are too far away for me to get more than a general direction once we get closer I should be able to find him quickly," Layla quickly explained.

Everyone but Martinez went silent trying gathering their thoughts. He had started to complain about the treatment that he was receiving until Amelia ordered him to shut the hell up. "What are we going to do with him?" Layla asked then after a seconded added, "If we take him with us he will betray us every chance he gets."

"I guess we will have to get him to Charles and let him deal with him," Andrew suggested not sure what else they could do with him. Andrew noticed has he made the suggestion that Martinez's relaxed and he actually got a small smile on his face. "Do you think that Charles is going to spare you? He will most likely encase you in concrete for betraying him," Andrew angrily warned.

"You are a fool whelp do you honestly believe that he will take your word over mine I have been an ally of his for centuries. Even if he did, I don't think he is going to risk his position for a couple parvulus do you. I will make a deal with you let me go and give me this cunt and I won't only let you two to live but I'll arrange to have your son returned," Martinez snidely offered with a large smirk on his face.

Andrew was just about to give him his retort when the phone rang. "Charles, good timing I was just going to call you," Andrew said into the phone.

"Andrew what the fuck is going on? What the hell have you two done and what were you thinking? I have reports claiming that you set a nightclub full of people on fire and you did it front of almost hundred witnesses. Lastly, did you kidnap or kill Martinez?" Charles angrily demanded.

"First of all we did what we had to do to survive. Yes, I did set a nightclub on fire but the only people in there were Amsu and his men. Martinez is out guest for the moment however, it may interest you to know that he is in bed with Amsu he has been playing you for a long time. Any other questions?" Andrew replied flippantly.

Layla couldn't believe that Andrew had spoken to Charles that way. Even when she enjoyed Amsu protect she would of never dreamed of provoking a lead enforcer in such manner, it was suicide. As she listened to Andrew talk to Charles, she began to wonder if she had a mistake getting involved. She was taking a big gamble going against her sire. She knew that if Amsu captured her she would die a very bad death.

"Andrew you have to understand there is no way I can protect you. You have kidnapped the head of the second largest coven in Central America who has connection you could hardly fathom that is the only reason Rodrigues hasn't killed him. You have to release him and get to my territory." Charles argued hoping to make Andrew see just how stupid this move was.

"Charles he is supporting Amsu against you. He has made a deal to be the head enforcer of all of Europe including the Former USSR and Rodrigues gets all of the Americas. On top of everything else it was Martinez that had my ex-wife killed," Andrew screamed the last part into the phone his control starting to slip. He took a couple deep breathes to calm himself then continued in a more sedate but no less intense tone, " He has to die and if I have my it will be a slow painful death."

"Andrew you can't kill him it would be signing yours and Amelia's death warrant. There would be no way I could protect you. I have to insist you release him immediately and return to Philadelphia. Please don't disobey me. If you have proof of your allegations then I will have him brought up on charges in the proper manner." Charles said in a tone that was more like an order then a request.

"Charles we are not your underlings we are your friends and that is the only reason I have shared the fucking information I have. Amelia read his mind and he was responsible for what happened to my human family including Jake being turned they wanted to draw me and Amelia out and now they have succeeded and they are going to reap the wrath of what they have sown." Andrew replied with finality to his voice.

"Andrew what the hell do you mean that Jake has been turned no vampire would turn a child. How Do you know he was turned and how did you find out? Lastly who was supposed to have done it?" Charles asked clearly shocked that a vampire would even consider turning a child. A turned child would never age or physically mature. That would mean the child that was turned would look and have the physical maturity of the age they turned and many times their mental development would be forever trapped at the age they were turned.

"Charles, Amsu forced Layla to turn him or he was going to kill him. She did it to protect him and while I am not happy that she did it, I will forever be grateful she did what she had to, to protect him. Before you ask yes, I do believe her," Andrew replied calming slightly. "Now are you going to hold this cowardly cocksucker or do I just kill him now? We're going to get Jake. And if anyone gets in my way may God have mercy on them because I won't. Layla had promised to help us retrieve him then we will work out what is best for him."

"Charles please believe we are doing what we have to and we will understand if you can't help us. Please do me one favor and protect Catherine, Brittney and Scott if something goes wrong," Amelia pleaded.

"Amelia that goes without saying. I will do my best to protect you two also please reconsider what you're about to do. I will work through other channels to get Andrew's son back. Please just get across the border and I will get you all to a safe house until we can get you back here. Bring Martinez with you form what you have told me we should have no trouble having him receive a proper punishment," Charles requested.

"Charles if it was Emma would you, could you leave?" Andrew asked.

"Alright Andrew I see your point. Then you have to dispose of Martinez and do it quickly before he can use telepathy to contact his people and lead them to you." Charles suggested not believing he was going to get involved with them. He knew it could be a disastrous mistake especially if they failed. He just prayed that they were right about Martinez and they could provide irrefutable proof.

"Charles I have him under control for now." Amelia said.

"Amelia, you all have to get rid of him and quickly he is too old for you to maintain control of indefinitely. To be honest I am not sure how you even managed to get him to begin with." Charles pressed hoping that they take his advice.

"Charles they got him by working as a team against him it was quite impressive. They must be a major asset no wonder you are willing to go to such extreme lengths to help them." Layla spoke for the first time. She was fishing hoping his comment would provide her with some kind of idea just how far Charles was willing to go to help them.

"Layla they are impressive and you are right I value their skills greatly but as Andrew stated earlier we are friends and I value that even more than their skills. Does that satisfy your curiosity?" Charles replied letting her know he knew what she was doing.

"It does Charles but I have to disagree with you about Martinez it would be better if we could put him on ice somewhere just encase we need a bargaining chip, dear brother," Layla replied. The last part was a playful snipe at him she knew he hated when she called him that.

"The problem with stashing him someplace is finding a location that would be able to hold him where he wouldn't be found. If you have a suggestion of one, I am all ears. I would hate to think he is able to communicate your plans to one of his people. If he is able to relay your plans to the other then your slim chance of success will be gone and you all will be walking into a trap," Charles quickly argued.

Layla turned towards Martinez and punched into his chest. She then reached in and ripped out his heart. She held up his still beat heart making sure that Martinez saw as she crushed it while she proclaimed, "That is for your part in making me hurt that precious child. Amsu you are next."

Martinez was setting their listening to the conversation they were having about him. He was relaying what he was hearing to the group of men that were following them at a safe distance. He was just about to protest while he mentally ordered his men to rescue him. He looked into Layla's hate filled eyes for a brief couple moments before he felt a sudden burst of pain in his chest and his eyes went out of focus. The pain subsided and his focus returned just in time for him to see his still beating heart being crushed. The last thing he heard was Layla's proclamation before oblivion took him.

Amelia and Andrew were listening to see if Layla knew of a place to put Martinez when much to their shock Layla punched into Martinez's chest then ripped out his heart and held in front of Martinez's eyes as she crushed it. Her actions caused the whole inside of the vehicle to get coated in blood. Amelia watched in horror as Martinez's corpse rapidly mummified. It was almost comical that the vampire was driving as if nothing had happened.

"Why the hell did you do that?" Amelia demanded her tone conveyed the shock she felt.

"What happened?" Charles asked through the cell phone that Andrew still held. He was shortly forgotten. As Andrew stared at the now lifeless body its blood pouring from the large hole in the chest.

"Layla just ripped Martinez's heart out of his chest and got blood all over the inside of the Jimmy." Amelia replied still in shock.

Andrew sensed the other vehicle closing in on them he knew they were Martinez's men and they wouldn't be pleased that their boss was dead. He waited until the car was right behind them and Andrew opened his door and shoved Martinez's body out hoping that the car would stop to take care of their boss. "Step on it," He ordered the driver who ignored the order until Amelia repeated it Andrew was pleased when the car that was pursuing them stopped to take care of the body.

Amelia had the driver make a few quick turns once she was sure they had lost their tail. She then ordered him to head southeasterly out of town. She had him stay off of the major highways and stuck to the surface streets. While Amelia was handling the driver, Andrew went back to Charles.

"So, what are you all going to do now? Rodrigues will have bounties out on you and Amelia within the hour, which means the Ubertas Venator will be hunting you and most likely he will offer a large enough bounty to get Vlad and his crew involved. Andrew you have to get back to my territory or I won't be able to help you at all. Please my friend I don't want to lose you and Amelia," Charles pleaded.

"Charles I still need to rescue my son and try to provide for some kind of life for him. What would you have me do?" Andrew replied as he tried to work out the best way to rescue his son and not get all of them killed.

"Andrew you have to understand this he is no longer your son he is a vampire. Chances are that if he aint already rogue he will be shortly the mind of a human adolescent isn't prepared for the life of a vampire. Think about the trouble you and Amelia had once you realized what you had become; now imagine going through it as a teenager. I know Layla was doing what she thought was best but it would have been better if she had let him die." Charles explained hoping he would be able to reach him.

"Charles he is my son and I refuse to give up on him. We will contact you once we are done." Andrew replied.

"Andrew then as much as it pains me to say this you are on your own. I can't risk everything to help you in this foolish endeavor. If you do this the only way you will be able to live a in peace is if you get proof of what Amsu was doing then kill everyone that is involved in the plan." Charles warned.

"Charles please keep Catherine and her family safe." Amelia requested.

"I will do my best Amelia you have my word on that." Charles promised.

Susan snatched the phone from Charles while glaring at him. "Andrew, Amelia if you need help you call me I won't abandon you. Fuck it I will have my people mobilized and we will meet you in Mexico City. Just please don't do anything till I get there." Susan said.

"Susan as much as we appreciate the offer we can't ask you to risk everything. Even once we rescue Jake, we will still have to run and hide. I am not foolish enough to think that we can face Amsu and win. Hell we will be lucky to survive long enough to pull the rescue off. Take care of Catherine and her family please." Andrew replied grateful for Susan's offer.

While Charles was waiting for his pissed off mate he went to his computer to look up Vlad's number. He may not be able to get directly involved but he sure wasn't going to abandon them. He noticed there was a message on the forums of the Blood Exchange. He quickly read it.

"Wanted Two Rogue Vampires reward of $125,000,000.00 each.

Amelia and Andrew Barnes who were sired by Diamond. Their human names were Andrew martin and Amelia Hensley. The two of them are extremely dangerous. Last spotted driving in an older model Blue GMC Jimmy in Tijuana. We have a report that they are heading towards Mexico City. If spotted please contact Eriko Rodríguezes Lead Enforcer of Mexico at 1-52-998-555-5555.

"Susan keep them on the phone and get in here now." Charles mentally screamed as he grabbed the phone and quickly dialed.

"Hello Charles, what can I do for you?" Vlad said smoothly. He was sure why Charles was calling to try to protect those parvulus of his. Vlad was already mobilizing his men for the hunt after all not only would he get the satisfaction for the sucker punch he received but also a large payday.

"Hello Vlad I'm calling in a favor. Stay out of the hunt for the Barnes." Charles requested

"Sorry Charles but that isn't going to happen. Even if they didn't insult me the payday is too high," Vlad replied.

"Vlad you owe me and just as a reminder they are still under my protection and if you anything happens to them I could forget an old promise of discretion in certain matter if I do I wonder who's bounty will be larger yours or theirs. Not to mention that in my grief I may accidently release the location of certain people you hold dear. Lastly, I may decide to take my vengeance on those you hold dear if I recall Anna is still here in Philadelphia." Charles threatened.

"Charles don't threaten me you do not want to make me an enemy over some pet parvulus. You know as well as I do that if you release that information Strigio would hunt you also for not reveling it to him before now. If you so much as touch Anna I will kill you myself." Vlad angrily responded.

"I am willing to risk Strigio wrath are you? I will have Anna staying with us as my guest if you try to warn her or get her out of my area I will place her in irons and lock her in a very dark cell and as far as your threat please come and try to kill me," Charles taunted. While he was talking to Vlad, he quickly wrote an address down and passed it to Susan as he telepathically said, "Tell Amelia and Andrew to go there and to please wait for my call. Tell them that I give my word of honor that this isn't a trap or a ploy to interfere with their plans I'm trying to help them. Lastly warn them that a $125,000,000.00 each bounty has been placed on their heads and that everyone knows where they are heading."

"My god! How are you going to protect them with that kind of bounty on their heads?" Susan asked with her mind. She then went back to Amelia and Andrew.

"Charles be reasonable even if I don't go hunting for them my men will and ..." Vlad tried to reason.

"Then I hope for your sake you can control your people because if I have to, you will pay the bill. One final thing for you to consider if anyone touches them, I will send Gloria to hunt them down and will give her a free hand on how she finds them. You may want to recall how she hunted her parents killers." Charles warned.

"Susan would never allow it and even if she did, why would Gloria care about them? They're nothing." Vlad retorted with a laugh.

"Vlad you really should keep better tabs on things. As soon as Gloria finds out about the bounty, she will be heading to protect them with or without permission. They feed her their blood to keep her alive when she was shot by that sniper. Susan for your information is mobilizing her people to go to Mexico and her plan is to help those two parvulus anyway she can. Did you hear we are mated now so guess who is going with her? So I guess I will leave Anna in Emma's tender care." Charles said in a low tone not even attempting to hide the implied threat.

"Charles neither my people nor I will participate in this hunt. You have my word of honor but know this we are done I will never help you again and if I find you anywhere near Anna I will use everything I have and every favor owed to me to bring you down . DO I make myself clear?" Vlad promised his anger barely contained.

"I understand but you understand this you have six hours to have you and your people out of my territory. Anna will be staying in Philly as my guest if you attempt to move her, I will kill her slowly and then come for you. She will be safe as long as you keep your people out of the hunt if they join she pays. Do I make myself clear?" Charles stated coldly.

"Anna leaves with me or I will personally track down your pets and make a gift of them to Rodrigues." Vlad threatened.

"Then I will see you in Mexico and Anna will be the one who delivers that file to Strigio along with a note explaining who she is and just how much she means to you." Charles angrily replied.

"You win Charles but if anything happens to her I will place such a large bounty on the heads of the people you love that it will make the one on your pets look small," Vlad angrily stated.

"Thank you for seeing things my way I appreciate your cooperation." Charles stated evenly.

CHAPTER 4

***

Charles knew that Amsu was the one behind the outrageous bounties either he was worried about something that Layla knew or more likely he was trying to force Charles to act to get his little war started. Charles' instincts told him to stay as far away from Andrew and Amelia as possible but he knew that it would be impossible with Susan's attachment to them. He carefully considered the best way to prevent the war Amsu wanted. He wondered if he could somehow negotiate with Rodrigues to get Andrew's son back. The only other option he could see was to start the dam war himself and try to minimize the scope of it.

Susan walked into the office where Charles was and took a seat across from him. She was pleased that she had succeeded in convincing Andrew to go to the address Charles had requested. She was slightly upset with herself for doubting her mate she should've known that Charles would never forsake a friend. She watched as Charles hung up the phone with Vlad and quickly dialed another number.

Andrew wasn't happy with Susan's suggestion about going to the safe house instead of going after his son but after she explained that, he was not only throwing his life away but also his mates he couldn't refuse. He knew it would take them just over nineteen hours to get to the address but first they had to lose their prisoner and get a new vehicle. Andrew had Amelia tell the driver to pull over and drop them off afterwards he was to drive straight to Philadelphia and go to Sanguinem on Water Street and Ask for Charles. He had her order him not to stop for anything but food and fuel. Finally, he was to use the blood in the cooler and not to feed from humans. Amelia repeated the orders to the Vampire and added he was not to be captured by humans or other vampires. The last thing she ordered was that he forget everything he had heard them say and then sent him on his way. While Amelia was giving the other vampire her instructions, Andrew called Susan and explained what they had done. She told them they it had been a great idea and hopefully he would act as a decoy and take some of the heat off of them. Susan said that she would have Gloria call them soon to see how she could help and she pleaded the he would allow her to help after some debate Andrew reluctantly agreed.

Less than five minutes later Andrew's cell rang. "Hello, yes I was expecting your call...No; that isn't necessary... Yes, we are heading for the safe house that

Susan suggested as soon as we get a new vehicle. Hang on a sec." Andrew moved the phone from his face to talk to Amelia and Layla, "Gloria said she will join us at the safe house. She suggested we try to keep as low of a profile as possible."

"Andrew, Gloria has many contacts down here perhaps she could suggest somewhere we could acquire a vehicle discretely. The contacts I would normally use will, without a doubt, sell me out for that kind of money." Layla said knowing that Gloria had an extensive network throughout the world she could use when she needed something discretely.

Gloria had heard Layla statement and thought for a few moments she had just the person. Donnie Marcus he went by the name Peppy He said it liked the name because it was memorable and defined his personality. She always teased him calling him Mr. Le' Pew after the famous skunk. She chucked to herself as recalled seeing Pepe' for the first time when she went to see They Were Expendable because she had a big crush on Robert Montgomery back then.

"Andrew, I know just the person to see. His name is Peppy, I will warn you that he is a bit of a flake but I trust him and he can get you anything you need. Tell him that Gloria is calling in a favor from Mr. Le' Pew. Here is his number." Gloria rambled off his number from memory and then quickly disconnected the call before Andrew could ask her anything else.

Andrew quickly called the number Gloria had given him. He waited as it rang a couple times and once the call was answered he heard a rather gruff voice demand," Who the fuck are you and how did you get my number."

"I am a friend of Gloria's and she gave me this number. My name is Andrew." Andrew replied hoping he wasn't making a mistake.

"Gloria huh? How would a parvulus know her?" The voice asked suspicious.

"Before I answer any questions, are you Peppy?" Andrew inquired.

"I am, now answer my question!" Peppy demanded. He was just about to hang up. He didn't like identifying himself to people he didn't know the only thing that caused him to pause was Gloria's name she was a dear friend and one of the few people he trusted.

"We are friends of hers and we need to obtain some discrete transportation." Andrew stated then quickly added, "She said to tell you she was calling in a favor from Mr. Le' Pew."

The phone went silent for several moments and Andrew had thought that he had made a mistake he was just about to disconnect the call and call Gloria back. "Andrew, sorry I had to clear the room. You said that you needed discrete transportation. To where? If this is who

I think it is I would imagine you need it for three people," Peppy responded his whole attitude had changed.

"You are correct about the number of people and yes I am Andrew Barnes. We need to get to out skirts of Mexico City," Andrew replied.

"That is no problem. Where are you now?" Peppy asked.

Andrew told him where they were and Peppy requested that they go to the bar and grill down the street letting them know that he was very familiar with the area. He had also suggested that they contact Gloria and have her meet them at a pub named El Caldero. He said to have Gloria meet them there at six in the evening in two days. He said that the driver he was sending them would be identified by the person walking up to Amelia and saying une belle rose pour une jolie femme and requested in a light manner that Andrew not attack his son. Lastly, he warned them that Rodrigues had everyone out searching for them and please be extra careful. Andrew thanked him for all of his help.

The three of them went to the bar he has suggested and took a table in the corner near the entrance. They had just placed their drink order when Amelia the sensation she was being watched. She surreptitiously looked around the bar until she spotted a woman she thought she knew that was seated towards the back of the bar. Amelia tried to recall where she had seen the woman with the toffee colored skin before she knew she was a vampire and even though she hadn't meant her personally, she knew her. She was just about to see if Andrew knew her when the woman turned her head and even though her hair was shorter, she recognized her.

"Dammit I think we were just spotted. Andrew look over my right shoulder. The third table past the support column and tell who is setting there," Amelia quietly said.

Andrew did as Amelia directed and saw her he instantly remembered her. "Fuck that is Flora, the bitch that sired Scott." Andrew exclaimed not believing their luck. Andrew was about to suggest that they try to get her out of here so they could privately deal with her when she suddenly rose and headed towards the restrooms with her cellphone in her hand, "Want to bet who she is calling?"

"I already know Rodrigues to collect the bounty." Amelia replied without even thinking. The place was too crowded try to stop her in the open. There would be too many witnesses and even if the humans didn't get involved, the commotion would draw other vampires into the fray in an attempt to collect the bounty.

"Go wait for me outback by the dumpsters. I will go fetch the bitch," Layla ordered.

"Layla that is too dangerous if Rodrigues' men get here you could be trapped." Both Amelia and Andrew said at the same time.

"I thank you both for your concern but I am going to be fine. If we don't stop her she may follow us and lead Rodrigues gorillas right to us." Layla responded with a reassuring smile.

Layla carefully made her way back towards the restrooms just before she entered the bathroom after making sure no one else saw her, she turned invisible and shielded her presence. She quietly slipped into the bathroom and heard the end of Flora's conversation make it clear that she was most definitely turning the three of them in she even had the gull to tell them to bring her, her money. Layla crept back to the door and locked it knowing no one would think much of it since quite of few of the local hooker used the restrooms to service their clients. She waited until Flora came out.

Flora finished up her call to Mr. Rodrigues she hadn't expected to get the head enforcer himself and was surprised when he came on the line. He had grilled her on how she knew the Barnes and she explained how they had stolen her Parvulus Scott. Once she convinced him that this wasn't a prank and that she really did know them he had promised her that his people would be there within twenty minutes and she would be justly rewarded.

She walked out of the stall with visions of how she would be spending her reward when she felt cold steel press against her throat. She heard a woman's voice whisper to her that if she tried to scream or resist she would be killed right where she stood. She couldn't believe her luck she had thought that Amelia had spotted her but Amelia turned back around and started making eyes with her mate again she thought she hadn't been recognized. She had left the table to prevent Amelia from getting a second look at her and when she got into the bathroom, she was sure she was safe and placed the call. "What do you want with me? I aint nobody," Flora stated in a weak whinny voice.

"I heard your conversation with Rodrigues and I know you reported us I even heard him tell you if we left to follow us. You are going to do exactly as I say or I swear I will kill you very slowly." Layla promised in a chillingly calm sickeningly sweet tone.

Flora knew she had to do as she was told or she wouldn't leave the bathroom alive. Her only hope was that Rodrigues' men would get there in time to save her. Layla had her arm tightly around Flora's waist while holding the knife to her throat as they walked out of the restroom. Layla did to make sure that Flora didn't try anything stupid like turning visible or yelling out in the middle of the crowd. As they were walking towards the door, she could see that Flora was looking for some way to get away but Layla was determined to make sure that didn't happen. She guided the two of them towards the dumpsters and her waiting friends the Barnes. Once they got close, she let the two of them come visible. "What are we going to do with her now?" Layla asked hoping that Amelia and Andrew would see reason and just kill her.

Amelia stood there for a minute or so thinking when she heard Andrew suggested they kill the bitch and be done with her. All of the sudden she had an idea that would not only take care of her but would serve as a warning that they weren't to be trifled with. "Allow me to rip every thought from the sorry bitches head and leave here as a warning for those who want to fuck with us." Amelia said with an evil smile. The fact that her eyes had gone black and were shinning was good indication that her baser side was in control.

"Y...you m... Mean t... That s...Shit is true. She can destroy my mind. Please have mercy on my and do not do that to me." Flora pleaded tears running down her face. Flora was afraid, hell she was scared almost out of mind. She fell to her knees and began to plead for mercy.

"You want mercy from me after you tried to turn my mate and myself into Rodrigues? You must be joking." Amelia sneered as she grabbed Flora by the hair and forced her to look into her eyes. Amelia eyes glowed brighter for a second.

Flora felt her head being pulled back by her hair and was forced to look into Amelia's eyes. She hadn't wanted to but as soon as she saw them, she couldn't look away She felt a tremendous amount of pressure in her head then she could feel her mind literally being ripped out of her brain. Her last thought was this couldn't be happening to me before everything went blank and everything that made the pile of flesh now lying on the ground Flora Anne Tamera was gone and all that was left was a vegetated hulk with no conscience thought. The only part of the brain that seemed to be working was the medulla, which is located in the brainstem.

Layla had heard that Amelia had the ability to destroy someone's mind but hadn't believed it. To say that she was impressed was an understatement. She looked down one last time and was still shocked to see the woman who had been pleading for mercy was now lying on the ground her eye fixed and dilated staring into space but seeing nothing. Her face was slackened and the only sound you could hear from her was her slow regular breathes. Layla had already tried to see if she could get her to respond with no success. She wanted to talk to Amelia more about what she had done but now wasn't the time. "We need to get out of here now," Layla urged. She watched as the Barnes followed her.

"We need to turn invisible and shield of presence and Andrew please call your contact and let him know about us having to move," she said as she turn invisible but willed herself to remain visible to both Andrew and Amelia. She noted that they had done the same. Unsure where they should go she headed them towards the center of town in hopes that it would throw off their Rodrigues' men knowing they would expect them to try to get as far away from the city as possible.

Andrew quickly called Peppy and explained that they had been spotted and had to leave the bar he redirected them to strip mall about five minutes away and told them that his son would be there waiting for them. He was driving a blue Lx. He let Andrew know that he had placed several units of blood in a cooler in the back just in case they needed it. The three of them arrived at the location and saw the Lexus parked in front of a burger joint. The three of them turned visible as they walked towards the vehicle so as not to startle the driver; once they got closer, they noticed that the driver was enjoying a burger while waiting for them. Just as they got to the vehicle, he got out and waited by the door until he saw Layla, his eyes narrowed and he quickly presented her with a single long stem rose and said with lust-filled eyes, "Une belle rose pour une jolie femme."

Layla stood there in shock he eyes were riveted to the young vampire. She forgot to breathe even as her heart felt as if it was going to leap from her chest. She could hardly believe after all of her years of searching she would find her mate now when her life was hanging by less than a thread she knew when she decided to go against Amsu she would most likely not survive and was at peace with that thought right up to this moment. "Merci, mais je crois que c'était censé aller à elle," Layla responded with a slight blush.

"Non, mon amour, il a toujours été fait pour vous." He gently took Layla's hand in his own and softly brushed her knuckles with his lips before continuing, "Excusez mes manières, je suis Fredrick Marcus."

"Je suis heureux de vous rencontrer monsieur. Je suis Layla," Layla responded trying to compose herself. After a brief pause, she continued now in English, "These are my friends Amelia and Andrew Barnes."

Fredrick took Amelia's hand and quickly gave her knuckles a light kiss then quickly released her hand. He quietly said, "Ah mademoiselle, the pleasure is mine I have heard quite a bit about you and your mate. I am Fredrick Martin but you may call me Fred if you wish and I am at your service," He then offered his hand to Andrew.

Andrew shook the hand that was offered to him and as he did, he took measure of the vampire before him. After studding him for a few moments and decided he liked him and that he was someone they could trust. He could tell that Fredrick had come to the same conclusion that he had and two of them could now relax.

"I would suggest that we all get moving before your friends show up here." Fredrick suggested.

Everyone loaded themselves into the SUV and headed out. Fredrick told them he would be using the back way he figured that everyone would be looking for them on one of the highways since they were not familiar with the area. Once he started out he offered everyone a burger he had figured they would be hungry. Fredrick and Andrew took turns driving, only stopping for fuel and food. The trip only took them a little over sixteen hours and they arrived a day early for their meeting with Gloria. Fredrick told them he knew of a safe place for them to stay at it was a bed and breakfast ran by some old family friends of his. He said that he trusted them with his life.

Fredrick took their and got two rooms He would be sharing one room with Layla while the other would be shared by Amelia and Andrew. Layla lead Fredrick to their room she wouldn't wait another minute to taste her mate. She quickly closed the door as she heard Amelia chuckle at her antics. The noise of the door closing hadn't died out when she started quickly stripping her clothes thankfully her blouse was a pullover or she would likely tore it off she pulled off her pants revealing that she had went commando this day. She turned back to face Fredrick standing there still fully clothed and started to stalk to him as a lion would go after a water buffalo she had the same hungry look in her eye yet for a different reason. She reached for his shirt and ripped it from his body then shoved him onto his back and quickly shucked him from his pants. She then pulled him back to his feet and gave him a soul-searing kiss. He could hardly believe she had managed to remove his clothes so quickly.

Layla quickly squatted in front of Fredrick and inhaled his member until her nose was buried into his thick pubic hair. She inhaled deeply relishing into his scent before she starting bobbing up and down for a few minutes then raising her head until just the tip of his cock was still in her mouth she slowly swirled her tongue around the head before she let it fall form her mouth. She smiled mischievously before using her tongue to trace the large vein that ran on the underside of his dick form the tip to his root. Fredrick started to wrap his hands into her hair trying to guide her back onto his cock. She looked at him and waggled her finger back and forth. "You have to show patients my delicious treat or I will tie you up and make you watch as I pleasure myself, then maybe just maybe I will give you some relief in a day or so," Layla playfully threatened.

Fredrick quickly released her head and moved his hands to behind his head. Layla made him wait as she slowly inspected his equipment taking great interest in his balls. She took them in her hands and slowly tested there weight. Fredrick was beside himself with desire he wanted to take control but something about the look of her eyes warned him that it would be a mistake for him to try so he stood there and fought to remain in control as she conducted a head to toe examination of him.

Layla squatted back down then started to pump her hand back and forth along the length of his rock hard member causing pre-cum to flow out of the tip. Layla watched the flow for a moment then used her tongue to gather as much as she could before making a big show of swallowing it. She took just the tip back into her mouth and slowly lowered her head down its length until it got to the back of her throat she then used her throat muscles to slowly draw the rest of his length into her throat then let her muscles massage his length.

Fredrick had never felt such pleasure in his life. He had more than his fair share of blowjobs but had never had a woman who could use her throat muscles in suck as fashion. He tried to warn him that he was about to cum and all she did was to cause her throat muscles to constrict increase the pleasure as he let lose his load straight down her throat. He couldn't believe how much he had shot. He felt his knees start to shake as his legs started to give out. He placed his hands on her shoulder to steady himself or he would have fallen on top of her. Once Layla was done, he pulled her up into his embrace and kissed her deeply tasting his offering to her it was a first for him.

Fredrick use the embrace to regain his strength once it had returned he gently lowered her to the bed. He slowly perused her body slowly savoring each and every inch. He was looking forward to taking the rest of eternity to learn every millimeter of her body and each of her secret places that every woman had that gave them that extra bit of pleasure. He started to trail kisses from her lips to her right earlobe. He took his time and explored her earlobe then trailed kisses across her chin to her other earlobe he swirled his tongue along the ridge of her lobe then kissed right behind her ear on her neck. Fredrick slowly kissed down the side of neck to her shoulder, which he nibbled across until he arrived at the point where her arm meant the shoulder. Next he kissed his way down to the base of her left breast he carefully nipped the top of her breast just hard enough to bring her to the point of pain. Fredrick looked into Layla's eyes and gave her playful wink. He used his tongue to make a few figure eights around the base of her breast on the fourth time around he stopped in the valley between her breast and deeply kissed her chest.

He licked his up her right breast to the nipple he drew it into his mouth and sucked hard on it for a few minutes, sending shivers down her spine. He then switched to the other nipple and used his teeth to tug gently on her nipple while swiping his tongue back and forth across the tip of the nipple sending a mixed single to her brain, the slight pain of his teeth tugging on her nipple mixed with tickling sensation of his tongue was only increasing her pleasure. He then switched back to the other nipple and sucked on it while tweaking on the nipple he had just used his teeth on. He alternated his mouth on each of her nipples a few times. He could feel her start to build towards her release just from his ministrations on her breast.

He next started to kiss his way down to her now sodden pussy he paused to explore her belly button using his tongue, afterwards he continued to his destination. Once he got to her pussy, he used his tongue to lick the length several times then used his tongue to trace the lips of her pussy. Fredrick next used his tongue to fuck her pussy. She was starting to quiver with pleasure so he decided to switch tactics. He latched onto her clit while he finger fucked her until her orgasm exploded. He didn't even slow his assault it anything he increased it by slipping his finger into her ass causing her to cum harder even before the first one had faded. He kept finger fucking both her pussy and her ass as he now used his teeth and tongue on her clit. Layla was bouncing so violently with her orgasm he could hardly keep his mouth on her clit. Finally, after her fifth orgasm she started to beg him to stop, she couldn't take anymore and all he did was look up at her and give her a wicked smile then redoubled his effort causing her to have two more huge orgasms before he relented. By the time he had finally let her have a break she was a quivering mass flesh that couldn't even produce a cohesive thought.

Fredrick's member was now as hard as steel. He slowly moved up and placed his cock at the entrance of her pussy. He gently pushed in taking his time to sheath his rod fully into her warm passage. He slowly withdrew himself about half way before slowly lowering himself back into her. He was going slow savior every inch of warm passage while driving her nuts at his slow pace. She tried to show the same patients she had demanded but after ten minutes of him slowly sawing in and out of her all the while teasing her mercilessly with his mouth she could take no more. She quickly used her superior strength to roll the two of them over and rode him as if all of the demons in hell were chasing her. She could feel herself building for another orgasm and just before it hit she bite deeply into his shoulder and savored every drop of his life essence he shared with her.

Fredrick found himself under Layla and chuckled. He was just about to tease her about her lack of patients when he felt the start of her orgasm. Next, he felt her fangs sink into his shoulder that caused his orgasm so he quickly sunk his fangs into her shoulder to enjoy her life essence. The two of them laid there together coming down from the most intense orgasm of their lives as their new bound snapped into place. Neither of them could have imagined the deep seeded connection they now shared and it was a bit over whelming for the two of them. Thankfully, the older innkeepers had recognized the look in Fredrick's eye and realized he would be mating this evening. So not five minutes after the two of them had finished there was a quiet rap on the door and the lady of the house stated that there was a warm carafe of blood and a bottle of champagne on the cart for them. Lastly, she congratulated them.

The two of them smiled and Layla used Fredrick's shirt to cover herself enough to retrieve the cart. She noticed that not only was there blood and Champagne but also some nibbles and long stem red rose in a crystal vase. Layla quickly rolled the cart into the room and poured each of them a goblet of the warmed blood. The two of them toasted east other and then drank the goblets of blood. After they finished the whole carafe of blood then went onto the Champagne and nibbles until they regained enough strength for round two.

Andrew had led Amelia to their room and as soon as the door closed, he dug out the laptop and looked up the address he had been given where his son was reportedly held. He saw that it was less than thirty miles away and he could have him and Amelia there in about an hour. He wondered if he should wait for reinforcements. He thought on it for over an hour running everything through his mind especially the risk to his mate but even with that risk he decided he had to try to rescue his son immediately and not wait for later. He looked at Amelia and noticed she had changed into a skintight black outfit that still allowed her freedom of movement she would require for a job such as this and smiled. He was so glad that fate had selected her as his mate. He quickly changed into a similar outfit before accepting the kukri and pistol Amelia had given him. He noted she had hid the same weapons on her while he changed. Amelia quickly wrote a note explaining what they were attempting to do and placed on the pillows.

The two of them turned invisible and shielded their presence from other vampires as they set out on their self-appointed mission. Andrew took Amelia into his arms and took off into the night quickly accelerated. Amelia closed her eyes and held on she had learned that it was better to just trust in Andrew ability to avoid an obstacles then to scream the whole way. It had taken them nearly an hour to get to the house where his son was being held. The house was a large rancher style house with a basement. They slowly circled the house to see where the exits were and if there were any visible guards. There were three exits front and rear of building that looked as if they went to the main floor and a basement door that had five steps down to get to. The rear door opened onto a large deck and was structurally the weakest of the doors. They had also seen four guards stationed on the rear deck all of them seemed to be human. Andrew could only sense two vampires in the building but for some reason he couldn't get an exact location on them something was interfering with his senses.

"Let me take control of the humans' minds and let see if we can get some intelligence on what we are facing on the inside," Amelia suggested mentally.

"That would be great but I didn't know you could seize four minds at once even if they're human." Andrew replied the same way curious if she actually could.

"I know I can easily do two. I have taken two vampire minds at once," Amelia replied using their bound.

"Love, let's stick to what you know for sure you can do. Now isn't the time to take any unnecessary risk. I will take care of the two on the left you can have the two on the right," Andrew replied telepathically.

Amelia nodded her head and the two of them moved into position. Without the need of a signal, they both moved at the same moment Amelia quickly seized control of the two men she had been assigned while Andrew just as quickly render the other two men unconscious. The men that Amelia had seized control of had little knowledge of vampires. They did know there were eight other guards on the main floor and six in basement. They were also told that the Middle Eastern man had left two days before hand but he had left a child in the basement. They had mentioned that there was a crazy acting gringo in the main bedroom, they were ordered to stay away from. Amelia ordered one of them to go into a deep sleep the other she told him he needed to use the bathroom then to return out here and join his friends in a nap. Amelia and Andrew turned invisible again while still shielding their presence as they followed the man into the house. They entered the dining room where four humans were playing cards. Andrew and Amelia quickly incapacitated them.

Amelia and Andrew looked around carefully. They saw the steps that headed to the basement. Now that Andrew was inside his senses seemed to clear up he could tell that there was a vampire on the other end of the house most likely in one of the bedrooms and the other one was in the basement. He also could sense two other humans on the main floor and three more in the basement. The two of them were glad that the other vampires hadn't sensed their presence yet it would make their lives a lot easier. They could hear a television playing at the bottom of the steps as they crept down the steps using the television to cover any noise they made by movement.

In the room at the base of the stairs were the four humans and a female vampire watching soccer on the television. They were playfully arguing about which team was better while the consumed a large quantity of beer. They could sense that they female vampire was as young as they were if not a little younger and she seemed more interested in the humans than anything else did. The humans appeared to be armed with a variety of handguns but didn't seem sober enough to use them effectively.

"I think if we get the drop on these morons they will most likely surrender without a fight. Do you think you could get control of her without too much trouble," Andrew asked telepathically taking advantage of their bond.

Since the humans had their backs to them, it was easy for the two of them to get the drop on them, which meant that the vampire was their only real concern. Amelia and Andrew withdrew their pistols in unison just before they came visible. The humans were caught by complete surprise, as was the vampire and before she recovered enough to do anything Amelia had control of her. "Ok gentleman let's keep this civilized so no one has to get hurt. All I want is my son, so tell me where he is and we will leave you in peace." Andrew said in a surprisingly calm voice.

All of the humans grimaced before nervously pointing to a door at the other end of the room. Amelia could sense that the female vampire was genuinely scared but couldn't pierce her shield to read her mind. Amelia was intrigued by the young vampire how was she able to protect her mind even when Amelia was able to take control of her. She even resisted Amelia command to lower her shield, normally once Amelia had control of someone it was total but with her Amelia's control was limited to preventing her from moving. The only other thing Amelia could sense was that the woman wasn't inherently evil she was just a young woman who was trying to cope with the situation she found herself in much as the rest of her family was in a way she sort of reminded her of Scott.

Andrew made his way to the door he was anxious to get his son just as he opened the door he realized that he couldn't sense his son. As he opened the door, all of the humans suddenly tried to make a break for the stairs to get out of there but Amelia was easily able to prevent them from leaving without serious injuries and now the humans were cowering on the floor trying to hide behind each other like a bunch of scared little kids. Now that the humans were subdued, Andrew opened the door and almost immediately fell to his knees as his strength gave out .He saw his son or more correctly his son's head setting on a shelf his eyes staring at him almost accusing him of not being there when he was most needed. Andrew human side retreated allowing the primal side to take reign. Andrew eyes goes black his lips thin out as his fangs extents and his skin draws up and turns leathery. Finally, his skin took on a deathly paler as his nails extended and sharpened into claw like weapons. He turned and started towards the cowering humans his lifeless eyes had almost a hypnotic effect causing the humans to freeze as their minds tried to comprehend the horror their eyes were seeing.

Much to her horror Amelia saw what Andrew had seen through their bound and was fighting with her primal side to maintain control she was concerned that if she didn't maintain control she would lose Andrew forever. Amelia tried to push into Andrew's mind to help him regain control of his beast but he was too enraged. She couldn't even reach Andrew human side and after several attempts, she realized that she had to let the devil have his due then hopefully once the primal side was sated she could reach Andrew and help him to regain control. Amelia sensed that the young vampire would somehow be important in the near future but she didn't know how so Amelia used her abilities to shield the young vampire from Andrew as she moved her to safe place and told her to stay there if she wanted to live. Luckily, the young vampire listened to Amelia's advice and stayed where Amelia had hid her.

Andrew methodically killed humans in the house taken time to enjoy their screams. He seemed to relish in their pain and no amount of pleading would sway him to spare them one ounce of pain. Amelia was afraid she had lost the Andrew she had come to know and love. She had been trying to reach Andrew but all she would sense was his overwhelming need for revenge finally after all of the humans had been drained Andrew arrived at the door where they had sensed the other vampire. Both Amelia and he could sense that the vampire was still in the room but seemed either not to sense them or not to care about their presence. Andrew ripped the door from the hinges before he advanced on the vampire who had his face buried into his hands and appeared to be weeping uncontrollably.

Andrew paused even in his current state something about this broken vampire was familiar. Finally, his primal side relinquished his control and allowed the human side to come forth. Now that Andrew was calmer and back in control he could sense the utter despair and self-loathing this familiar vampire felt. "Tony?" Andrew asked then paused until Tony looked up. He then continued with tears streaming down his face, "What the fuck happened? Why did you kill Shannon? I trusted you to protect her and Jake and you let them die! How could you do that?"

"I tried Andrew I really tried to stop but that other man made me do it if I could of killed myself I would of done it but all I could do was watch myself rape and murder the woman I love. Please just destroy me I cannot live with I have done." Tony begged while on his knees.

"Why should I ease your suffering you murdered Shannon and allowed my son to die also?" Andrew screamed in anger. Andrew grabbed Tony by his throat and slammed him into the wall with such force that he not made a large hole in the drywall but broke several studs in half.

Tony offered no resistance to Andrew he really wanted to die and felt he deserved every bit of pain that Andrew inflicted on him. "Andrew I am so sorry I tried to resist him but I couldn't stop myself from following his orders. I felt like I was watching a movie of my body doing exactly what Carlos wanted me to do. There was another vampire their he was from the Middle East he seemed to be in charge but it hurts so much when I try to recall anything about him after I left Carlos he had me doing horrific things to other people. He said to tell you that there was a message for you by Jake." Tony quickly explained as he continued to sob.

Amelia wrapped her arms around Andrew as she softly whispered, "I am so sorry my love. I know it hurts but I need you, please don't leave me." Amelia held Andrew in her arms allowing him grieve for his ex-wife and his son until he calmed down. She kept her eyes on Tony she was almost sure he was sincere but didn't want to let her guard down totally just in case. Once Andrew had calmed she mentally said, "Love I know you are hurting but we have to release him. It wasn't his fault and he is suffering. If you don't want to do it then I will."

Andrew nodded his head slightly giving Amelia his blessing to end Tony's suffering. Amelia moved in front of Tony and gave him a small smile. "Find peace." She said as she quickly removed his head releasing him to find the peace he desperately needed.

Andrew caught Tony's body and as he slowly lowered it to the floor, he made a silent promise to avenge him. Andrew went to the room where his son's head was left and found a Disc with his name on it. He placed it into his pocket to watch it later on. He then carefully picked up his son's head so he could bury it properly. The whole time he was lovingly wrapping Jake's head into the blanket he had found he was begging him to forgive him for not being there.

Amelia had retrieved the young vampire from her hiding place Amelia had the girl help her with Tony's body. While they were working, Amelia had found out that the girls name was Paola and that up to two weeks ago she was a nineteen-year-old college student that didn't believe that vampires existed now she was one. She told Amelia that she had been turned by accident by Tony and that Amsu told her to just wait there and keep the humans in line and someone would be coming to take care of her.

The three of them placed the bodies by the front door and was just about to leave when they heard a SUV pull up out front of the house. The three of them turned invisible and Andrew and Amelia shielded their presence against detection. A moment later, they realized it was three vampires who had arrived and Andrew peaked out the front window, saw a very worried, and pissed off Gloria standing there.

Gloria walked towards the residence flanked by Layla and Fredrick all three of them on alert, unsure of what they will find. Gloria could understand Andrew's inpatients but was still perturb by his lack of faith in their friendship. She had managed to arrive earlier then she had anticipated and called Pepe to find out if he knew where they had decided to stay. He hadn't, however once he informed her that Fredrick was chauffeuring them she knew exactly where he would choose to stay. The two of them had had a fling some years back it had only lasted a few months but it was a wild few months.

Once Gloria had arrived, she was pleasantly surprised to learn that Fredrick had found his mate in Layla. Gloria had meant Layla a few times through the years and had always liked her even if she didn't fully trust her. She first considered allowing Fredrick and Layla to stay at the bed and breakfast but the two of them wouldn't hear of it; arguing that it was very likely that the Barnes had gotten in over the heads and that she would need all the help she could have. At first, Gloria was a bit skeptical but after Layla announce that she could no longer sense Jake and that he was dead Gloria knew that things were going to be very bad and they all would be extremely lucky if Andrew hadn't crossed over.

Layla wanted to avenge her fallen parvulus by hunting Amsu down and making him suffer however, she knew she would be committing suicide if she tried to hunt him alone. Layla knew that Amsu had become vile soulless creature but to harm a child without cause was a new low for him.

As she tried to fathom what Amsu had hoped to gain by killing Jake. She couldn't believe that Amsu actually thought he could get his foolish war by causing Andrew and by extension Amelia to go rogue. She was sure that Charles was too smart to go to war over a couple of Parvulus no matter how fond he was of them.

Andrew, Amelia, and Paola stepped out on the porch after coming visible. As Andrew stood beside his mate, his posture was tense while his eyes slowly scanned the area looking for any possible threats. Paola hid behind Amelia as soon as she saw the three new vampires' faces. She was afraid they would end her no matter what Amelia had promised.

Gloria slowly ran her eyes across the group noting that Andrew's eyes had failed to change back before stopping on Paola. Gloria could tell that she wasn't even month old and was scared out of her mind. Gloria took a deep breath trying to relax herself. "Andrew, are you alright?" Her voice was full of concern. No sooner than the words left her mouth, she realized her poorly chosen words and cringed.

"I am nowhere near alright!" Andrew retorted harshly. He took a deep breath trying to reign in his erratic emotions before continuing, "That bastard killed my son, he killed my ex-wife, he tried to have my mate killed, and you ask me if I am alright?"

Amelia quickly wrapped her arms around Andrew and tried to push into his mind to calm him but was having very limited success. Her concern for her mate was evident on her face she had no idea how to help her mate; he seemed to be sinking deeper and deeper into the darkness. She knew if she didn't' turn him back she would lose him forever. Amelia's eyes pleaded with Gloria to help her.

"Andrew, I am so sorry that this happened and I swear that we will avenge them. But please Andrew let go of the hate it will destroy you like it almost did me and I care for you and your mate too much to see that happen." Gloria softly said as she slowly approached once she got close enough she wrapped her arms around both Andrew and Amelia. "We will get through this together.

Andrew please let go of the hate it will only destroy you and those that love you." Gloria pleaded in a whisper.

Andrew stiffened when Gloria first hug him but quickly relaxed as she spoke to him. He knew she would understand his burning need for revenge. As he listened to her words, he thought back to the story she had told them about her early life. He quickly realized that if he weren't careful he would go down the same path she did. His baser side was confused by the strong emotions coming from his other half and that gave Andrew the opportunity to wrench control back. He took a deep breath and closed his eyes soaking up the strong feelings of love and the support that the two women were offering. "Thank you," he said softly his voice tight with emotion.

Amelia breathed a sigh of relief when she looked and she saw that Andrew's eyes had gone back to their normal hazel color. She hugged Gloria and whispered her thanks before she turned her attention to Paola who was trying to make herself as inconspicuous as possible. "You have nothing to fear from these people they're our friends." Amelia softly explained to her.

"I apologize for interfering, but the Federales are going to be here soon and we need to remove the bodies of any vampires and be gone before they arrive." Fredrick cautioned as he closed his cell phone.

Fredrick and Layla loaded up Tony's corpse while Andrew carefully placed the blanket containing Jake's head in a box and placed it in the back of the truck next to Tony's corpse. Then everyone loaded themselves into Fredrick's SUV and he headed south-west out of the city. As Fredrick hastily drove out of the city, Gloria dialed Charles number to update him.

Charles had received a call from Gloria informing him and Susan that Andrew and Amelia had taken matters into their own hands and decided to raid Martinez's compound on their own. Charles Immediately called the airport and had his pilot ready the seven-sixty-seven and have flight plan to Mexico City approved for them to leave within the hour.

Twenty-eight minutes later, they were in the air racing towards Mexico with twenty of his top security people. Charles and Susan were in the air heading for Mexico City. Charles knew that all hope for a peaceful solution was ruined and that Amsu would have his war. His objective now was to minimize the war and keep causalities down on both sides. Catherine and Scott had wanted to come but Susan had refused to allow them because of Brittney Lynn.

Charles left Emma and Neil in charge of things in Philadelphia. He was worried that Amsu may attempt to strike at Catherine or Brittney in order to draw both Amelia and Andrew out. He couldn't help but wonder why Amsu was so fixated on the two of them he knew that He wanted revenge for Diamond however this was unlike Amsu, normally he would have had them killed outright and not play these games. The Amsu he knew would never; no matter what expose the vampire nation to the humans, they were far too dangerous. While he was setting there trying to make sense out of Amsu actions they had received a call from Layla letting them know that Amsu had killed Jake. He felt sorry for Andrew's loss but in his heart, he knew it was for the best, after all he had never seen a case where a human child had successfully made the transition. A human child was not emotionally or mentally ready for the requirements of being a vampire. Charles knew that eventually Jake would have had to be put down for the safety of everyone.

As they were leaving, Layla suddenly remembered just how young the Barnes were and asked cautiously, "Andrew are you sure that you drained all of the humans dry?"

"I drained them completely and there is no chance of them returning from the dead," Andrew replied in a tight voice. His eyes however glowed showing that his baser side had gleamed immense satisfaction from draining the humans dry. The problem with his eyes it also showed that his baser side was still very close to the surface and was ready to retake control of Andrew.

"Andrew I am sorry but I had to ask before we got too far away. You are new to this and your emotions are clouding your senses," Layla offered sincerely.

"I understand," Andrew responded managing to give her a small sad smile. His baser side retreat slightly.

Gloria hung up from talking with Charles. "Charles and Susan are going to meet us in Cancun. They suggested that we stop at Susan's facility in Oaxaca. Andrew they will also take care of the remains of tony and Jake," Gloria explained and braced herself for his response.

"I could care less what happens to Tony's body but I want to have a proper funeral for my son," Andrew angrily demanded his eyes starting to darken.

"Andrew, I understand but we can't get caught with a severed head in the car. I promise you they will treat both of the remains with the upmost care and respect and once we get back to Philadelphia I will help you to plan a remembrance for both Jake and Shannon" Gloria tried to reason with Andrew. She understood how he felt and could remember what it was like for her when she was dragged away from her farm before she could bury her parents, in fact it still bothered her to this day. She managed to come to grips with and even forgive herself for her other acts but that one action was still an open wound on her soul.

"Are you sure they will treat him properly?" Andrew replied in an unsteady voice as tears formed around his eye. As much as he hated to have to admit that Gloria was right, he knew that she was. The only way he could attempt to get vengeance for his son was to allow the people at Susan's facility to handle Jakes remains: he couldn't say even to himself dispose of his remains. He swore to himself that he would see Amsu and the others hand for killing his son.

As they road Andrew had his eyes closed praying he that this was some kind of terrible dream he had barely made peace with the fact that he would outlive his child by realizing that his son would have a long and full life. Now because Amsu and this other vampire he no longer had that comfort and he wanted them to suffer. His baser side was whispering promise of blood and pain for those who had hurt him if he would just let him out and Andrew was leaning towards letting the monster have his way. He was just about to give into the pain when a tiny whisper in his mind asked him, " do you want your child's legacy to be the cause of a war were millions will die needlessly or do you want your child's death to be the catalyst for change? You can help to stop this madness before Amsu goes any further."

Andrew couldn't believe what he was hearing he thought for a moment, that he had lost it totally. Then he recognized the voice it was his grandfather. "I don't know how to stop this even if I wanted to," He responded to his grandfather.

"Andrew you have wanted to be a cop since you were old enough to say the word so be what you were meant to be a cop. Find the cocksucker that did the actual killing and make him tell you who to after next. In addition, you have a couple advantages you have never had before first the bastard doesn't get Miranda Rights or a lawyer and second that rather attractive young lady beside you. Now stop moping around and go get the bastard," the voice demanded.

Andrew said a small prayer of thanks for his grandfather's gentle persuasive ways even though he knew his grandfather had been dead for over ten years he knew his grandfather had come to help him at least in spirit. Now that the voice of his other half had been silenced, he started to think on how to proceed. He knew he had to build a case against Amsu and Rodrigues so that they could live in peace. If he failed to make a case against them, he and the rest would be hunted for all of eternity.

Several hours later, they stopped at a small gas station and while Fredrick was fueling the SUV, the rest of them went into the store next to the station to buy snacks and drinks. While they were checking out Andrew noticed the headlines of the morning newspaper and quickly added it to their purchase. It read, "The bodies of the

Martinez drug cartel found drained of blood." The paper then went on to describe that the bodies of several high ranking members of the Martinez cartel had been found earlier this morning all of the bodies had been drained of blood by some unknown means. The Article also reported that Santiago Martinez mutilated body was found in the house. The paper had stated that the police and Federales are investigating the attack as a territory dispute.

Early the next day, the SUV containing the five friends and Amelia's young guest Paola, pulled up in front of Susan's facility. The outside looked like an old adobe house like hundreds of others in Mexico but the inside looked like a modern medical office building. Gloria explained that as far as the locals knew the building bought blood for research purposes paying between fifty and two hundred peso per pint of blood the rarer the type the more money they got. Even though blood was blood as far as for nutrition many vampires claimed that, the rarer blood types tasted better so they were willing to pay extra for it. Paola didn't realize how hungry she was until the smell of the blood hit her she had not feed for the last three days and she was starving. Without her realizing, her eyes had changed and her baser side was now taking control.

Amelia who was closest to Paola sensed the change and quickly took control of her mind to force her to maintain control of herself. Amelia quickly realized that the poor girl had even less of an idea of what being a vampire then she had had and she knew if it hadn't been for Andrew, she wouldn't have survived her first night. As Amelia scanned her mind, she saw glimpses of an older vampire that had been controlling her; she could sense that the vampire was powerful. Whoever this man was he was the one who had been controlling things and he had left right before Andrew and her had arrived at the house, which made Amelia wonder how he knew the two of them were coming. The vampire looked and sounded as if he was from the Mediterranean area. After careful deliberation, she decided to keep this knowledge to herself for the time being.

Andrew could sense that Amelia had seen something in Paola's mind and now was keeping it from him. He had attempted to peak at what Amelia had saw but he shield was too strong for him to breach. "Amelia what did you see?" Andrew asked anger and hurt laced his voice.

Before she could respond, a young vampire walked into the office area and called out, "I am looking for Detective Andrew Martin please."

Andrew didn't respond at first surprised to hear his old job title. The young vampire repeated his name, "I am Andrew, who are you and what do you want?"

Andrew responded his gaze freezing the young vampire in place.

"I am Felipe, Mr. Martin," Felipe replied nervously. He swallowed involuntarily as he attempted to calm himself every instinct he had was screaming for him to run and get as far away from this place as he could. He nervously glanced over his shoulder towards the exit and noticed that a rather attractive blonde vampire had blocked his exit. He slowly looked towards the only other exit, which was the window to find it was also block by an equally attractive Middle Eastern vampire. He could sense that she was the oldest vampire in the room. He knew he was trapped and he cursed himself for being swayed by the large amount of money they had promised to pay him. Twenty-thousand Pecos just to deliver a box but his greed had made him reckless. He swallowed once more then held out the box he was carrying offering to Andrew. "I was told to deliver this to you," He continued weakly.

As soon as Andrew accepted the box Felipe, quickly turn and started to walk towards the exit hoping that the blonde headed woman would allow him to pass. He had gotten a few steps when he heard an inhuman roar behind him and he turn just in time to be lifted by his throat and carried to the wall. Felipe closed his eyes and quickly prayed to survive this day with his head in tact just as he was painfully driven into the wall.

Andrew quickly examined the box it was an aluminum box with a thick rubber seal around the edge of the top. He cautiously released the two catches and cracked the box open when the scent of blood overwhelmed him not just any blood but Jake's blood. His baser instantly took over and launched towards Felipe grabbing him by the neck crushing his airway while driving him into the wall. Andrew heard the satisfying crunch of bones breaking. "Who sent you?" Andrew demanded.

Filipe tried to answer but his throat was too badly damaged. He struggled to get Andrew to loosen his painful grip to no avail. He found himself being repeatedly slammed into the wall and each time he heard and felt more bones being shattered. The pain was becoming overbearing and he looked around the room praying to find someone to help him. He locked eyes with black female whom seemed to be Andrew's mate and pleaded for her to help him with his eyes.

Amelia was the pain and anguish in Felipe's eyes she notice him trying to use his eyes plead to her for help. She laid her hand on Andrew's arm and pushed into his mind trying to calm him while she softly pleaded, "Andrew, My love he won't be able to answer you if you kill him. Please put him down and let him recover so he can answer your questions "

Andrew ignored her at first but after she repeated herself, a few times, as she started to massage his shoulders he slowly started to calm down, which allowed him to regain control. Once he was calm, enough he released the young vampire and stepped back, into Amelia's waiting arms. Andrew glared at Felipe as he fought to maintain control of himself.

Felipe was on his knees while trying to focus his energy on healing himself fast before Andrew lost control again he feel Andrew's eyes drilling holes in the top of his head and for the first time since he was a child he was afraid. He looked into Andrew's black soulless eyes and saw his own death. After what seemed like a couple of lifetimes, Felipe throat healed enough to allow speech. "I was promised twenty thousand Pecos to deliver the box to you. I had no idea what was inside it was just a job. I meant you no harm please senor let my go," Felipe pleaded his voice raspy from the damage that was still healing.

"Who gave you the box?" Andrew commanded.

"I don't know his name. He was almost as tall as you, had a tan complexion with black hair and he spoke with an Italian accent. I was to meet him at El Resto Del Vaqueroin four hours to collect the rest of my money." Felipe explained hoping he would live to collect the rest of his money.

"That is a bar on the west side of the city," Fredrick said before Andrew could ask.

Andrew listened to the young vampire and couldn't detect any lies. He glanced at Amelia who subtly nodded. Andrew pointed to a chair and asked, "How would you like to make five thousand American and four units of blood?"

"That depends sir on what you want me to do. I don't do murder for hire." Felipe replied shocked. A moment ago, he was sure he was going to lose his head and now he is being offered a job by the man that he thought was going to kill him.

"No, I don't want you to kill anyone. All I want you to do is go to your meeting and point the vampire that was going to hire you out to me. I will take care of the rest. Lastly, I will also make sure the he pays you what he owes you as an additional incentive," Andrew explained.

"He will kill me if I set him up," Felipe Nervously replied.

"He will never get the chance to. Amelia and I will be standing right beside you. Amel..." Andrew started to explain his plan when he was cut off.

"He will sense the two of you and we will all die," Felipe quickly interrupted.

"He won't be able to sense us . Amelia and I will keep you safe you have my word on that," Andrew pledged.

Felipe believed that Andrew was telling the truth, as he believed it and he felt bad for him after hearing that his child was murdered, but he just didn't believe that the two of them were strong enough to do what he claimed they could. The vampire that had contacted him to deliver the package was old he was older then everyone in the room with the possible exception of the Middle Eastern woman and she didn't seem to have the power that the vampire had had.

Andrew could see that Felipe was scared and was unable to make up his mind. "Felipe you are free to decline the offer but please think about it before you do. While he is deciding why don't the rest of us see what is in the package," Andrew suggested.

Felipe watched as the rest of them moved to the package and he saw that he had a clear path to the exit. He also noted that no one was paying any attention to him so he took the better part of valor and left as quickly as he could. The money that he was promised with what he had saved was enough to give his family and himself a fresh start in America.

Andrew opened the package and found a large envelope inside. He was just about to open it when Felipe made his break for the door. Gloria turn to stop him but Amelia gently laid her hand on her arm and shook her head.

"Let him go," She quietly said with a sigh.

"We already know when and where he is meeting his contact," Andrew stated with a chilling smile. Andrew turned back towards the box, once he opened the box; he found several photographs of his son, a disc and a note. Andrew looked over the photos with tears running down his face. Even in the photos, he could see that Jakes primal side had taken control His features were drawn and his eyes were black. Jakes face and shirt were covered in blood he looked like some kind of rabid animal Once Andrew got a hold of himself he opened the letter and read it.

Dear Mr. Martin,

I first must offer my condolence for your child. It was unfortunate that he had gotten caught up in these events and alternately had to be put down. I have enclosed a picture of him for you. The disc show why he had to be put down.

I have managed to convince my associate that the death of your human wife and child has balanced the scales and as such, I am given you one chance to leave with your lives. If you and your mate leave Mexico and disassociate yourselves form Charles Black and his minions then you have my word of honor we will never bother you, your mate. We will also remove the bounty that was issued on the two of you. This offer is also extended to your mate's first and her mate and child.

The disc that was left with Jake is for Charles Black I would greatly appreciate if you would make sure he receives it no matter what you decided. If you have already tried to play it and saw the message then I am sorry for repeating myself. If not the disc is encrypted so that only Charles will be able to start it.

Sincerely,

ZA

Andrew handed the letter to Gloria since Amelia had already read it over his shoulder. Andrew placed the CD from the box into the player on the laptop when Paola started to panic as part of her memories started to return. "Please do not watch that sir. It will do you no good," She begged as tears poured form her eyes.

Amelia wrapped her arms around Paola in an attempt to calm the frightened young lady. "It will be OK dear .Andrew won't hurt you." Amelia softly said while she started to rock the young vampire.

"You don't understand I know what is on the disc," Paola mournfully cried. She then whispered where only Amelia could hear, "It includes the boy's death."

Amelia hadn't been blocking Andrew and he heard what Paola had said through Amelia and his bond. He had suspected that the disc may contain Jake's death but he had to watch it nonetheless, he had to see if he could see the man that had murdered his son. Andrew came over and kneeled down beside Amelia and Paola.

"Where you there when they made the video?" Andrew gently asked.

"I was forced to film it. I tried to resist doing it but he was too strong for me he made the other vampire do it, the one that was left in the house. He enjoyed watching the poor man beg him not to make him do it. The cruel bastard laughed as he forced him to behead the child. Paola replied in a shaky voice. Her eyes were hooded as she recalled the memory. She suddenly grabbed a wastebasket as everything she had ingested came back up. After several minutes, she finally emptied her stomach. Once she was finished, Fredrick handed her a bottle of water so she could rinse her mouth out.

"Who was too strong?" Amelia asked as she rubbed young girls back trying to calm her.

"He was... I cannot remember it hurts too much," Paola replied her voice strained from the pain in her head.

"Relax; stop trying to force the memory." Andrew gently but firmly demanded.

"I can help you to remember without causing you pain you just have to relax and trust me. I promise we won't let anyone hurt you," Amelia swore.

"What do I have to do?" Paola asked. She knew that there was something important she needed to tell them but it she couldn't remember what it was she could recall the older Middle Eastern man perfectly his name was

Amsu. He had left a couple days before Amelia had showed up. She now remembers filming the horrible murder of the boy but everything else was just out of her reach. She could tell her memories were there but she couldn't get to them.

Amelia had Paola take a seat to help her to relax. She took the young vampires hands in her won and locked eyes with her. Amelia gently started to probe her mind until she ran up against Paola's mental shield. "Relax and lower your shield. I promise I won't hurt you." Amelia softly promised.

"I don't know how to lower my shield," Paola responded her voice thick with despair.

"Close your eyes look into your own mind and find the area that is responsible for protecting your mind from others. You will know it once you find it most people see it as a wall or some other form of a barrier," Layla explained.

Paola was quiet for several minutes as she looked for the area that Layla had described. "I have found it looks like a vault door. What do I do next?" She asked.

"Simple open the vault door and invite Amelia in?" Layla softly replied.

Amelia patiently waited while Paola lowered her defense never pressuring her. After Amelia managed to gain entry, she began to go through her memories until she ran into a block. Amelia easily probed the block but found it stronger than the one that Richard had had. She carefully led Paola around the block then allowed her to take the lead. Paola memories flooded back to her now and she quickly came to the realization that her memories had been false. Now that she knew the truth, Paola started to share her real memories with Amelia. She knew that ZRA was actually Ziaran Alessio and he was sadistic bastard who took great pleasure in torturing Tony and Paola. Ziaran was the one who ordered Tony not to kill Paola because he had wanted her. He had repeatedly raped and sodomized her over the first two weeks of life as a vampire. He had also limited her feedings so that she would remain weak and complaint. Her saving grace had been when Amsu had shown up with Jake. Amsu had forced Ziaran to feed her and allow her to regain her strength before he was allowed to start raping her again.

Amsu hadn't wanted to leave Jake in the care of Ziaran and only did so after Ziaran had sworn the he would protect Jake and allow no harm to come to him. Contrary to the memories that Ziaran had planted Jake wasn't rogue quite the opposite he was adjusting well to being a vampire and was looking forward to seeing his father now that he knew he was alive. Jake had overheard a conversation between Amsu and Layla about Amelia and Andrew. Layla was trying to convince Amsu that Amelia and Andrew would be assets to their cause and that Jake would assure their loyalty however, Amsu wanted Jake as a replacement for Diamond.

Ziaran saw Jake as an impediment, so he used Tony to kill Jake. Amelia watched Paola's memories of the killing and it was nether quick or merciful. Jake had suffered several hours of torture at Ziaran's hands before he had Tony remove Jake's head by twisting it off.

Amelia was so shocked by she had saw she hadn't realized that she had been sharing everything she learned with Andrew who was standing there still with tears flowed freely down his face and Anger burning deeply in his eyes. When she finally realized what she had done she quickly looked into Andrew's eyes fearing that he was losing control but found not an out of control vampire but a very pissed off dad that would have his vengeance and it would be a very slow and painful death for Ziaran. Amelia quickly calmed when she saw that Andrew was very much in control even with what he had seen she just hoped that Andrew would stay in control.

Amelia relayed what she had seen to everyone else while Andrew took a few minutes to recompose himself. Even he was surprised how calm and control he was in light of what he had witnessed. Once he had fully recomposed himself, he began to plan their next move. His knew his revenge would have to wait as much as it pained Andrew knew that he had to capture Ziaran alive and in shape to talk however as his baser side reminded him repeatedly that left a lot open the he could do. The thought of removing Ziaran's arm, legs, and especially his fangs; which never grew back once removed; delighted Andrew. He wondered if Charles would allow him to bury him up alive.

"Gloria could you please contact Charles and ask him for all of the information he has on Ziaran Alessio. Please tell him to hurry we have to leave here in less than an hour. Layla and Fredrick could you please figure out some place that Paola will be safe while we collect Mr. Alessio." Andrew requested.

Gloria quickly called Susan's number. "Susan we need all the information you have about a vampire named Ziaran Alessio." Gloria said as soon as Susan answered the phone without any of their usual banter.

"Why would you want to know about him? He had been dead for over sixty years," Susan responded with certainty even if she was clearly confused by the question

"Susan he was the one who had Andrew's son murdered. He is working for Amsu," Gloria replied as her own confusion set in. How could Susan be so wrong?

"Gloria that is impossible Charles witnessed his death. Ziaran was torturing and killing young humans in the Boston area and attracting way to much attention to us. You were on holiday so Charles personally hunted him down with Neal and Vlad. Ziaran had led them on a merry chase until they trapped him in a small cabin on the outskirts of Ottawa. They attempted to get him to surrender but after he wounded Neal they used plan "B" and set the back of the cabin on fire hoping to force him it didn't work and they found his charred remains after the fire burned out," Susan explained.

"Susan Amelia saw him in Paola's memories, the young vampire she rescued from Rodrigues's safe house..." Gloria started to argue.

"Ask them to describe the vampire" Susan demanded cutting Gloria off.

When Gloria asked Amelia for a description of the vampire, she had seen in Paola's mind Amelia held her hand out for the phone. "Hi Susan; He is about six two, one hundred-ninety pounds with shoulder length black hair. His skin was olive color and he had well defined but not over muscular body almost like a swimmer. The one thing that stood out in her memory was a ring it had a stranger stone or crystal that was dark red and it almost seemed to glow. He was constantly either tapping it as if he was bored," Amelia paused in her description trying to recall if there was anything else, she could think of.

"Amelia can you describe the stone any better or perhaps ask, umm, Paola if she knew what the stone looked like, not the color, but the shape," Susan asked clearly surprised but the mention of the ring.

Amelia closed her eyes and concentrated on the ring for a moment, "It was shaped like a skull with fangs."

Amelia answered. She could clearly see it in her mind. She went through Paola's Memories and could see the Ziaran greatly valued the ring one time Paola had accidently touched it while he was raping her. He immediately stopped and over the next few hours, he took great pleasure in breaking every bone in her hand several times, as he yelled at her for soiling his ring by touching it with her filthy hand. She was unworthy to look at the ring.

"That is him. He is a very powerful psychic with no conscience. He enjoys torturing and using inventive ways to murder people. He was turned by Vhald's youngest sister when she thought he was her mate. He took the ring from her after he tortured and slowly tore her apart. Amelia please wait for Charles and me before you all go after him," Susan explained her concern evident.

"Susan I am not sure what Andrew has planned but we have Gloria, Layla, and Fredrick to help us. Once Andrew lays out the plan I will call you back," Amelia finished and handed the phone back to Gloria. Susan and Gloria talked for a few more moments before hanging up.

Andrew waited until he had everyone's attention, "The only way I can see us having a chance for long term survival is to bring irrefutable proof to Charles to present to the other enforcers of Amsu's plans and our best option for this is to capture as many of his cohorts alive as possible," Andrew started to explain.

As Andrew was explaining his plan when the cell phone that Amelia had been using rang, "Hello," she answered wearily.

"Amelia let me talk to Andrew it is important," The unknown female caller demanded, her Middle Eastern accent evident.

"Who is this?" Amelia quickly countered.

"A friend, now if you all don't want to die in the next twenty minutes put him on," The mysterious caller retorted harshly.

Andrew took the phone from Amelia he had heard the conversation clearly. "Who are you and what do you want?" Andrew sharply demanded.

"I am your guardian angel, my dear and I am just warning you that you have about two dozen heavily armed mercenaries heading for your location and I seriously doubt they have your best interest in their hearts. I would suggest you get out of sight since they have the exits covered," She stated then paused for a moment. Andrew was just about to ask why he should trust her when she continued, "There is a panic room behind the supply closet to your left get everyone in there, and I will cover you. I promise that after I take care of these people I will explain everything," The mysterious caller hung up the phone right after she finished not giving Andrew a chance to question her.

Andrew listened to the unknown caller trying to gauge if she was being honest and though he couldn't detect any deceit, he was wary. "How do I know if you are telling the truth?" Andrew asked harshly.

"Believe me or not it makes little difference. Therefore, you decide either let me do the job I was asked to or get in my way and I will stay a spectator, Your Choice!" The mysterious caller retorted.

"I believe her," Amelia said telepathically.

"Alright we will go into the safe room," Andrew agreed reluctantly.

Once the manager heard Andrew agree, he told his other employees to head into the room. "Elena, I want you to lead everyone through the escape tunnel. I will bring up the rear." Augustine quietly ordered. He then announced to everyone, "Follow Elena she will lead you through the tunnel to safety."

"What about you?" Gloria asked. She liked Augustine; they had become good friends over the years.

"I will be right behind you I just want to secure the sensitive data before I leave. I will join you in a couple minutes," Augustine promised.

Gloria reluctantly entered the safe room and no sooner then she cleared the doorway then the door slammed closed behind her and the time lock snapped into place. Gloria cursed knowing it would be twelve hours before the door could be opened. Elena moved the shelf and started the procedure that would open the door to the escape tunnel. The procedure would take her about twenty minutes to complete if there wasn't anyone in the tunnel; if there was someone in the tunnel then they were effectively trapped because the exit door wouldn't unlock without the proper code which none of them possessed.

True to the mysterious caller's word, twenty heavily armed, rough, looking vampires entered the waiting area. The leader who was just over six feet tall and looked as if he just stepped off the front of Solider of Fortune magazine stepped slightly in front of the others. "We are here to bring in the fugitive vampires. Either produce them or we will tear this place apart and find them." He demanded in a menacing tone.

"Sir, I would request that you lower your voice this is a place of business. Now how may I help you?" Augustine spoke in a very businesslike tone without a hint of fear.

"I am here to affect the capture of the renegade vampires that are with Andrew Martin and Amelia Hensley. You will turn them over or we will remove you from our way and then tear the premises apart till we find them." The leader threatened as he places his hand on the butt of his holstered pistol.

'We both know that is an empty threat. All of the enforcers have signed an agreement that Susan's businesses are neutral grounds and if you cause any trouble in here all of you would be hunted and put down before you could collect your reward," Augustine replied in a calm but assertive manner.

The leader calmly removed his pistol form its holster and pointed it at the' Augustine's head, "Andrew if you do not show yours..." He started to say when the top of his skull disintegrated into a spray of blood and brains. The leader's body fell to the ground like a sack of potatoes. For a couple of a heart beat everything was quiet except for the sound of falling glass then everyone of the mercenaries moved at once trying to take what little cover there was before silence reigned again. After a few minutes, the phone rang. Augustine still in shock answered it after the second ring out of habit. He listened for to the person on the other end of the phone then put the call on speaker.

"Ladies and Gentlemen I thought you would like to know who is going to kill you. My name is Dafne but you may know me better by my pseudo name Le' Mirage I believe it was your former Employer whom gave me that handle. Hello Rafael," Dafne said with a chuckle.

"Dafne why are you involving yourself in this mess they are only a couple out of control parvulus?" Rafael asked nervously.

"Rafael my sweet I am going to miss our talks but I will indulge you one last time. Up to an hour ago, I would have said because you were taking my prey but I received a call from two old friends both of them asking me to protect these people one of them happens to be the first of one of the ladies you have trapped in there and the other caller was her mate. Both of them offering me outrageous amounts of money to protect them, not that their money is any good with me, but I had to ask Susan why she was so hell bent on protecting them. After she explained, I have decided it is a worthy cause and signed on to assist them." Dafne explained.

"Fuck," Rafael stated without realizing he said it aloud.

"Yes you are my dear. Oh by the way the three snipers that you had on over watch are taking a very long nap," Dafne said nonchalantly.

"Dafne, My dear can we please come to some kind of understanding? I don't want to die or watch my team die," Rafael requested.

He knew that if couldn't convince her to make a deal or they would all have a very bad day. He cautiously glanced at his surroundings trying to figure out her location when a red dot appeared in his right eye for a scant moment. Rafael quickly dove back into cover cursing himself for making such a rookie mistake.

"Looking for me my dear," Dafne taunted with a hardy laugh. Then her voice the turned cold as she continued, "I will indulge your curiosity. Did you see that tall building about eight hundred meters out .You know the one that you set your sniper on well I am sitting next to his cold corpse. O' that was his laser sight, not mine I detest those things."

There was total silence for a few minutes a couple of the mercenaries thought that she had hung up the phone. When one of the mercenaries asked using hand signal, "Want me to go out the back and try to slip around behind her?"

"Good plan," Dafne said with humor tinging her voice, "All you have to do is make it to the door. Are you ready to try?"

"How the hell did she know," The mercenary said before he realized he said it aloud.

"You can either run for it or die where you sit Vinnie. You have five seconds to start your run," Dafne warned.

"Please..." Vinnie said before she interrupted

'One thousand one," Dafne started.

Vinnie stay in cover! She hasn't got a shot," Rafael ordered sharply.

"One thousand two."

"One thousand three."

The man took off as she said four and just as he reached the rear door, he heard One thousand five then heard the glass shatter. He then felt a sharp pain in his chest. The last thing he saw was bloodstain spread across the front of his shirt as the darkness of oblivion took him

Rafael tried to stop Vinnie from running, he knew exactly what Dafne was doing. She was scaring him into breaking cover. He knew she didn't have a shot on Vinnie so she fucked with him until he broke cover and gave her the shot. "Why are you being a bitch? You could have proven your point without killing Vinnie," Rafael asked angrily.

"Two reasons on I wanted to make my point, as you call it, crystal clear. Secondly I hated the bastard since he killed Winthrop," Dafne replied showing no emotion.

CHAPTER 5

***

While Rafael was listening to her answer, he looked around wondering how she saw Vinnie's hand signals. He knew there was no way she should have been able to see them from her perch. He slowly scanned the room when he saw the camera above the counter and made it inoperable with couple of rounds from his Sig. "Without breaking cover take out those fucking cameras," He ordered sharply. He thought about taking out the lights but decided it would be a wasted effort.

"Are you happy now that you think that I am blind to what is going on in there?" Dafne asked sounding almost bored.

Rafael was trying to figure a way out of this situation he knew that Dafne wouldn't let one of them live it would be a mistake on her part if she did and that was something Dafne didn't do often; make mistakes. He was the manager hiding behind the counter trying to make himself as small of a targeted as possible. He pointed Sig at the man, "come here," He ordered.

Augustine hesitated not wanting to move until a round from Rafael's Sig slammed into the counter less than an inch form his head. Rafael placed Augustine so that his body acted as a shield against Dafne; making it next to impossible for her to get a clear line of fire on him. He started to dial Rodrigues number even though he dreaded making it. Rafael knew it would most likely cost them most if not all of the reward but he saw no other way of walking away from here alive.

"Rafael who would you be calling I hope that you aren't thinking of calling Rodrigues because if you did I would be forced to take more drastic action we both may regret," Dafne said.

"Like what Dafne? We both know you aren't going to let us leave here and forget about the whole thing," Rafael replied.

"What makes you think that?" Dafne asked her tone sounded almost bored.

Before Rafael could reply his call was answered, "Who is this?"

"My name is Rafael Antonius, Mr. Rodrigues; my team and I have the parvulus ..." Rodrigues heard Rafael starting to explain when the phone made a loud screeching sound just before it went dead.

Daphne maneuvered to where she could get a clear shot on Rafael. The wall that was now between her and him was of little consequence the rifle she used could pierce a half inch of plate steel and still have enough power to knock a man off his feet. She used her thermal scope and aimed for the hand that was by his head. Daphne checked the camera feed one last time to make sure no one had moved and she took a slow deep breath calming herself and slowing her heart. Once she was sure she was in her zone, she gently squeezed the trigger making sure she was between her own heartbeats so as not to affect the trajectory of the round.

The round left the barrel of the rifle at one thousand meters a second and easily cut its way through the wall speeding towards it intended target. Less than a heartbeat later, the round passed through the phone Rafael was talking on and plowed it way through the upper part of his right cheek exiting through his lower jaw of his left side and finally coming to stop in his left shoulder after shattering his collarbone. Rafael let out a gabbled scream of pain before collapsing. The only sound that was heard for several seconds after that was Rafael's labored raspy breathing inter mixed with him choking on his own blood.

"How did that call work out for you Rafael?" Dafne asked with a chuckle. Then her voice turned icy as she continued, "The next one of you that even thinks of making a call will die. He was my one warning."

"Dafne, its C.P. I am going to go check on Raf, please hold your fire," Cherie said in her calm but sultry manner before she rose and slowly walked towards her fallen comrade. Cherry checked over Rafael's wounds while they were grievous they weren't life threatening she knew that he needed blood to assist in the healing process. Cherry was raised in a small Celtic village where she like her mother before her was the village healer.

Cherie looked around trying to see where the manager of the facility had gotten to. She had lost track of him in the confusion after Rafael had been shot, no one had expected Dafne to be able to target them through a wall. She saw Augustine lying on his stomach about a meter from her and kicked him in the foot just hard enough to get his attention.

"I need a couple units of blood please," Cherie, pleaded.

Augustine looked at her as if she was crazy there was no way he was going to move. He never thought he would be in this situation where he was being threatened after all no one in their right mind would go against one of Susan's facilities it was pure suicide. He had never been an overly brave man he preferred to avoid conflict not that he was a coward but this was beyond anything he had ever experienced. The only reason he had confronted the mercenaries in the first place was that he naively thought that they would leave as soon as he reminded them who owned the business. Augustine was about to tell the woman no, but the look on her face made him want to help her. He nodded then quickly then glanced out the window hoping that he wouldn't be shot. He slowly rose and walked towards the cooler where the blood was stored.

After convincing the Employees from the Exchange to stay hidden near the exit of the escape tunnel Andrew, Amelia and the rest slowly made their way back to the building. They stopped just outside of the area where the other vampires could sense them. "Gloria and Fredrick wait here while Layla and Amelia try to work their way to the rear of the building. I am going to try to work my way around front and find my guardian angel once I do, I will call you each group, and we can have a conference call on how we want to rescue Augustine," Andrew ordered.

Andrew then turned to fulfill his part of the plan when Gloria grabbed his arm stopping him, "Andrew I think we should call Charles he had to be the one to enlist your guardian angel. Think about it who else would have known we were there and have the resources to acquire someone like her on such short notice?" Gloria quickly suggested.

Andrew paused for a moment then sighed, he should have thought of that himself, but the anger he was trying to hold at bay was clouding his judgment. He realized he had to keep his mind clear of the anger that was threatening to engulf him or he would make a mistake that would cost him one or more of the most important people in his life. Andrew took a deep breath and slowly released it attempting to center himself "You are correct; I should have thought of that myself, Sorry" Andrew quickly apologized.

"Andrew, you have nothing to apologize for. You are holding up much better than any of us had expected you to. You know we are all in this together and however this turns out I'm so glad I am with you and Amelia," Gloria exclaimed full of emotion before giving Andrew a sisterly kiss on the cheek.

While Gloria was helping Andrew to calm down Layla took out her phone and dialed the familiar number. She waited for the person on the other end of the line to answer, "Hello big brother I need to know if you sent someone to help us and if you did how can we contact her." Layla knew that her calling Charles big brother irritated him but she never could resist even though she knew it was a bit childish of her.

"Yes Layla, we did send someone to help you but why do you need to contact her?" Charles inquired before answering her question. He learned to ignore her calling him big brother long ago in fact now he sort of looked forward to her little tease not that he ever admit it to her.

"Augustine refused to go into the tunnel with us and is now trapped in the exchange with the mercenaries. We want to coordinate with your people to rescue him and then try to catch up with Ziaran." Layla answered hoping he believed her. She knew that Charles and her relationship was stressed at best. She had always been fond of Charles but Amsu had warned her about trusting Charles claiming that he would only use her to farther his own goals and quickly discard her once her purpose had been served. Though she no longer believed Amsu, she still was wary.

"Layla it is Daphne helping you. Her number is 011-972-4-555-5612. Don't worry about Ziaran, Susan and I will take care of him. Please let Andrew know and once you settle thing their please call me so we can arrange to meet to plan out the next stage of the operation."

"OK, Charles hopefully we will be calling you soon," Layla said before ending the call. She then handed Andrew her phone and repeated the number Charles had given her.

Andrew dialed the number while trying to decide what he was going to say, After the fourth ring he heard a rather annoyed sounding feminine voice, "Who the hell is this and how did you get my number?"

"I thought that a guardian angel always knew when her charge was contacting her," Andrew quipped.

"I am glad you managed to extract yourself from there. Now what may I do for you?" Daphne responded sounding amused.

"First of all thank you for all of your help, you saved our asses. Next how can we help to rescue Augustine?" Andrew inquired.

Dafne considered telling them that she would handle the extraction and for them to get as far from here as they possible could however after her discussion with Susan earlier she knew they would just attempt a rescue without her and most likely getting Augustine and a couple of them killed in the process. "I was considering offering them a chance to leave and hope that they would take it. I am almost sure that Rafael will call Rodrigues however we should be long gone before he is well enough to make that call." Dafne explained.

"Sounds like a plan, what do you want us to do?" Andrew asked.

"Hopefully nothing, I have a feeling once they know that you all have managed to escape they will be willing to leave without a fight," Dafne responded. Then paused as she worked out the final details of her plan, "Andrew do you think you all can safely make your way to the building I am on?"

"I could if you could tell me which building you are on," Andrew replied with a chuckle.

"I am across the street and to the left of the front door of Susan's place. There is a back door." Dafne responded in a much friendlier tone.

Andrew led the rest of them back the way they had came until he was a few blocks away he then made a wide circle towards the building that Dafne had indicated that she was on as they approached the rear of the building Andrew saw several large vampires about to enter the building and quickly moved to intercept them. As soon as he came into range of them being able to sense him two in the rear turned towards them and Smiled, "It looks like we hit pay-dirt boys."

The other three vampires turned and smiled as they fanned out to face Andrew. Amelia and Gloria quickly moved to Andrew's right side while Layla moved to his left. Fredrick stepped from behind Layla to move to her side when the lead vampire recognized him and his smile quickly dropped form his face and a look of concern that bordered on fear over took his expression.

"Fredrick what the fuck are you doing here with them?" the lead vampire bellowed out. His voice was full of false bravado that the rest of his features lacked.

"I am here to protect my mate and her associates," Fredrick stated nonchalantly.

"Then you and your mate are free to go all we need are the two parvulus and the one called Layla. So you and your mate are free to go," The lead vampire offered.

"My mate is Layla," Fredrick replied his eyes narrowing in anger.

"In that case we will let her go and bother you no more but the parvulus stay." the man offered.

Fredrick paused as he considered his response making Andrew wonder if he was going to accept his offer.

Meanwhile across town Ziaran walked into the El Resto Del Vaqueroin a few minutes before he was supposed to meet the young vampire that he had hired to deliver the box to Andrew although he had no intention of paying him he couldn't allow Felipe to live and since Andrew had failed to kill him he would have to do it himself. He had just started to head for a both in back corner when he heard, "Hello Ziaran, long time no see."

Ziaran cringed as he recognized the voice he slowly turned towards it and his worse fears was standing less than six feet from him. He swallowed hard and quickly turned and froze as he heard, in a menacing heavily Russian accented voice, "Going somewhere?"

Ziaran color drained from his face and his eyes went wide in shock the one vampire he feared the most even more then Charles was standing in front of him. He cursed himself for not paying more attention to his surroundings it was a mistake that only a parvulus would make and now it will cost him his life and he knew it wouldn't be a pleasant death. He glanced around to confirm what he had already known there would be no escape for him he noticed by each exit including the windows there we several of Vlad's men and he imagined that Charles had his men stationed around the outside of the building as an added layer of security.

Ziaran remembered Vlad's Sister Alina and how innocent she was which was surprising considering what she turned out to be. He hadn't known that she was a vampire and thought she would be a good time. Since it was apparent that she was rich he thought he ride the gravy train taking whatever he could get and then once he tired of her he would dispose of her in a fun way like he had all of the others. He smiled to himself has he thought of the night she had announced to him the she was vampire and he was her mate. At first he thought she was playing so kind of game but was quickly convinced when she bit him and started to drink his blood. After he changed it took him a few years to realize just how weak and dependent she was. It felt as if she was a millstone tied around his neck one which he relished removing after all he had it all now money, strength and best of all immortality. He loved the look on her face when he started tearing her apart piece by piece. He recalled Alina's final words, "Ziaran, you can't be doing this to me. I am your mate." Even now it was funny to him just how stupid Alina was.

A quick rap to the back of his head brought him back to the present. He turned and faced the man that would ultimately relieve him of his life and smiled. "Hello Brother long time no see," Ziaran cheerfully taunted . He knew his mental powers were of no use to him the three vampires that surrounded him were far to strong for his powers to work.

"I am no brother of yours." Vlad harshly retorted with a snarl as he shoved Ziaran forward towards Charles. Vlad couldn't believe it when Charles had called him and informed him that this bastard was still alive. At first he truly believed that it was some kind of trick to get his aid but once Charles had said that it was just a courtesy call because they had once been allies he knew that Charles wasn't trying to deceive him. What surprised Vlad even more was when Charles had offered to allow him to be in on the capture and he would allow him to hold and ultimately deal with Ziaran however he saw fit as long as he kept him alive and in good enough shape to testify against Amsu and Rodrigues.

He knew that Charles knew it was rightfully his place to decide Ziaran's fate but after the earlier altercation between the two of them, he was almost sure Charles would deny him that honor and would of dealt with Ziaran himself. He knew he now owed Charles a debt one the Charles would never collect on and claim that he didn't owe. Vlad was looking forward to getting

Ziaran back to his home where he could start to repay him for all of the pain he had caused his family.

Charles and Susan took a seat in the both next to where they were standing and waited for Vlad and their guest to have a seat across from them. Charles watched as Vlad roughly shoved Ziaran into the both and took the seat next to him blocking his escape route. They all set there a few minutes that seamed like hours staring Ziaran who defiantly stared back at them the smug smile never leaving his face.

"Hello Charles, I hear congratulation are in order. Please allow me to buy a bottle of bubbly so we can properly toast your mating," Ziaran expounded like the three of them were old friends and they were here to celebrate.

"I am afraid that the company has soured my stomach and I will have to decline having a drink with the likes of you," Susan sourly riposted. She was beginning to wonder just how deranged Ziaran was. He had to know he wasn't going to enjoy what was left of his pitiful life.

"Ziaran, I will give you one chance to die easier all you have to do is tell me who in my organization is helping Amsu and Rodrigues," Charles offered. He was hoping that Ziaran wouldn't realize that his promise was empty. Charles had no doubt that Vlad would make him suffer long and hard for his crimes before he finally disposed of him.

Ziaran looked as if he was going to accept Charles deal and had even started to speak when his expression hardened, "Charles you must think me a fool that deal gives me nothing. Give me your word of honor that you will kill me quick without torture then I will not only tell you who the traders are but will also give you the location of a file with enough proof to not only condemn Amsu but also all of his cohorts. Do we have a deal?" Ziaran asked.

Charles set there considering his options on one hand that file if it existed would be all of the ammunition he need to go before the council to justify his actions and also save Andrew and Amelia but that would mean he would have to break his word to Vlad. He glanced at Vlad who was staring at him his expression unreadable but he remained strangely quiet.

Charles decided he had to do what was best for all and just prayed that he was making the right decision. "Here is my final offer Ziaran. You will give me the file and any other information you have. You will also forfeit all of your assets they will go to your surviving victim. I won't have you killed slowly like I planned but will allow you a trial. That neither Vlad nor I will be the judge but I will be the one who selects the judge. you will be held by an someone of Susan choosing until you are tried but for this you will have to agree to testify against your former compatriots before the enforcer's council. If we have a deal I want a blood pact now," Charles demanded his expression was cold and the power that he had allowed to come forth had everyone on edge . Charles cut his left hand and held it out waiting to see if Ziaran would accept if not then it fall to him and Vlad to try to break Ziaran and get the information form him.

A blood pact was an ancient right in which two vampires would make a deal guaranteeing it with their own blood and failure to follow the deal to the letter would result in the death of the offending vampire. The death was said to very painful and slow it would take weeks to months to give them the chance to make good on the deal during that time the vampire wouldn't be able to feed and would slowly start to decay as if they were a corpse. The pact was rarely used and the last recorded time it had been used was in the late seventeenth century. Kristin McClain was the leader of a large coven in Southern England and had made a pact with another coven's leader not to attack them which he did almost a century later destroying the coven but invoking the curse of the blood pact. He had been so thorough that not member of the clan had survived that he could attempt to reestablish the deal with so he spent the last painful months of his life trying to find a way to break the curse.

"Charles you can't do this," Susan exclaimed in shock.

Ziaran quickly ripped his left hand open and grasped Charles' lest hand sealing the deal. "I agree to all of your terms as stated," Ziaran happily stated as he felt the slight burn of the pact taking place.

"We had a deal Black," Vlad angrily protested as he stood to leave the anger in his eyes burning deeply.

"I am truly sorry Vlad but I had to do what is best for all. I promise I will make this up to you," Charles promised.

Vlad snorted and turned to leave he had thought that Charles was an honest man but he was proven wrong. Worse of all he had forgiven Charles for his earlier call and thought they would become friends as they were before and now Charles had done the injustice to him. He was beyond incensed and would have his revenge if it took a millennium.

Susan locked eyes with Charles for a moment before rising. "Charles not only have you betrayed Vlad but also Andrew and our child have you forgotten what he did to Neil. I am leaving don't try to follow me," Susan said angrily as she stormed out of the door following Vlad.

Charles sighed he hated disappointing her but he had little choice when the welfare of his people was at stake. "Your information better be good as you claimed or I promise you that I will make you wish you died from the blood curse," Charles threatened.

"It is better than good in fact let's go to my suite and I will give all of the information required to fulfill my end of the deal," Ziaran suggested. He started to rise and noticed that six of Charles's men had appeared around him.

"They are here to protect you, I wouldn't want anything to happen to you at least until we are done, "Charles said. He then gestured for Ziaran to follow his men

Charles quickly lead everyone to the van he had had his men bring to the front of the club. The security men kept Ziaran moving and had him in the van quickly not giving anyone a clear target. Charles was glad that he had Kirk with him, ever since Mitch had died Kirk had stepped up and taken over Mitch's duties while maintaining his own since Charles hadn't had time to find a replacement for Kirk's old job.

Kirk had already been told he was the next head of security for Charles and his family. Andrew and Amelia were now head of security for Charles' businesses and also tended to handle personnel issues like the one with Christina Morehouse. He was glad that the two of them had taken those responsibilities off of him it made his life easier.

Charles paused suddenly and got a far away look in his eyes before he stepped into the vehicle with a sigh.

"What's a Charles mate abandon you?" Ziaran asked with a sneer.

"No she is just upset with me because I had to break my word to Vlad. She just let me know she was going back to our hotel and we would discuss my action later," Charles said not really answering Ziaran.

"I wish I could say that I was sorry to cause you so much trouble but we both know that was a lie," Ziaran replied in a smug tone he seemed to relish in Charles discomfort.

"Just remember my old friend I never promised that I wouldn't kick the shit out of you ,so if I were you I shut the fuck up," Charles threatened his eyes darkening.

"Charles we wouldn't want to kill me and invoke the curse least not till you got your precious information," Ziaran quickly reminded Charles.

Ziaran remained quiet for the rest of the ride a small fact that Charles was thankful for he had to decide how best to proceed from here. He knew that his relationship with Vlad would be strained for the time being but it was a necessary evil and he would make it up to him. He was worried about his other friends mostly Andrew right now he was sure that Andrew had to nearing his breaking point and if he did reach it then the distasteful job would once again fall to him. His stomach soured as he thought of Lenard whom had been his closest confidant; the two of them were closer then most brothers and he had to put him down. Charles wasn't sure he could kill another close friend and remain sane. He stilled missed Lenard and guessed he always would.

He knew that the events of Lenard's death had played a part in his decision to delay mating with Susan and most likely would of prevented him form not doing so if hadn't been for Andrew and Amelia. He because whom he is had placed his family and closest friends in more danger then ever before and he prayed that he was making all the right moves to keep everyone safe but he wasn't sure that their was even a right move.

Charles was so lost in his thoughts he failed to realize that they had arrived at Ziaran's hotel until he heard Kirk ask him how he wanted to handle things here. Charles forced all of the other issues to the back of his mind and thought for a moment before answering.

"Kirk have Andrea take his team up and secure Ziaran's room, Lisa's team will set up a perimeter around the vehicles then you,me and Lenard will escort Ziaran to his room once everything is secure . Lastly have the vehicles manned just in case we have a make a quick exit," Charles order knowing most likely Kirk had already had the arraignments in place.

A couple of minutes later kirk announced that everything was ready. Charles took the lead with Ziaran close on his heels Kirk and Lenard were about a half of step behind Ziaran. Kirk was slightly to his left and

Lenard to the right. The way the three of them had him covered with the additional guards creating a corridor it made it highly unlikely that an assassin would be able to get a clear shot at Ziaran.

"I feel like the president having all of you so willing to eat a bullet for me," Ziaran cheerfully taunted.

If Ziaran was going to make any other remarks he quickly changed his mind after Kirk gave him a sharp punch in his kidneys. Ziaran turned to protest but one look at Kirk he decided that it would be better to keep him mouth shut. The four of them quickly got to Ziaran's room and were greeted by two of Andrea's people standing on the door . Charles nodded to Mike and Peg as he went through the door he knew that they were both good at their job and were part of Susan's personal protection team when she traveled abroad.

Andrea greeted Charles as he entered the room, "Charles the room is secure. I stationed Trevor on the balcony. Les and Jorge are watching the elevators and stairs. We are on open mikes on channel six," Andrea said.

Charles quickly nodded his approval before turning to Ziaran, "Well where is the data?" Charles demanded.

Ziaran walked over to the bed and lifted the mattress in the center was a large manila envelope with two disc and a flash drive inside of it. "Charles you have to insert the flash drive then the disc. Once the flash drive decodes the disc it will prompt you for a password Alina61223," Ziaran instructed . He knew that Charles would recognize the date it was the date he had turned.

"Kirk get someone to bring us a laptop quickly," Charles' ordered. Normally he would of used please and thank you but Ziaran was really getting under his skin; just his presence was enough to push Charles to the point that he wished he hadn't made the deal with him but he had so he knew he had to tolerate it him for a bit longer. With in ten minutes Charles was reviewing the file that Ziaran had turned over to him and he quickly scanned the list of contacts and agents Amsu had working for him not only with in Charles and other enforcer's organizations but also with in the human community.

Charles suddenly stopped at one of the names as he reread it twice he felt ill when he read it. Amanda Rose Green had been hired to be Emma's Nanny when she was child and had became a close friend of the family she now acted as Charles head of household. He quickly called Emma and gave her the names of the people that were listed on this file and told her to take them all into custody. Emma had a hard time believing that Amanda had betrayed them and said she would interrogate her personally.

Ziaran reflected, while he waited while Charles was on the phone, he knew that most likely he would be executed but he was sure he would be granted a quick merciful death compared to what Vlad or Charles would have done to him. He held on to a small bit of hope that he may get prison instead even though in his heart he knew it was foolish but either way he had manged to escape endless hours of very painful torture and for that he was happy. Ziaran waited until Charles was done with his call to his daughter then handed him two more flash drives, "Here are all of my financial records as per our deal."

Charles had his people go over the room with a fine tooth comb making sure that Ziaran had indeed turned over everything. He had his men pack up all of Ziaran's belongings to take with them all told it had taken them almost two hours to go through everything. Charles then lead the group out through a side entrance of the hotel.

Ziaran quickly realized as they approached the Vehicles that it wasn't Charles people that were standing by them but Vlad's and began to worry. He watched in horror as Susan stepped out of the lead Escalade with a smile. "Charles, what is going on? Remember the pact," Ziaran nervously stated.

"I am following the pact. I said that Susan would select the person who was to act as your jailer and that neither Vlad or myself would judge you. I never said that Susan wouldn't select Vlad to act as your jailer. Don't worry my old friend he knows he can't kill you and you have to be able to testify in front of the council of enforcers," Charles replied with a hard cold smile.

"This is not fair you promised that I wouldn't be tortured and wouldn't be turned over to Vlad. I trusted you,you bastard," Ziaran ranted maniacally.

Charles let him rant for a few minutes then calmly explained with a smug smile gracing his lips, "First of all I never promised that you wouldn't be tortured. If you recall I said Susan would chose your jailer, I never even hinted that it won't be Vlad in fact I strongly suggested to her that she select him. I cannot think of a better jailer to give you everything you deserve. Lastly I have already decided who will set in judgment of you. Would you care to guess who and I will help you along it won't be Vlad or Myself as I stated for the pact."

"Let me guess your mate," Ziaran replied his voice barely above a whisper. He knew the rest of his days would not be pleasant and wished he had listened to what Charles had said a little closer but once Charles had said he would be held by someone of his mates choosing he was hooked and now it was going to cost him everything.

"Nope, I decided to allow Andrew will judge you. I can't think of a better person to sit in judgment of you. How about you Vlad?" Charles asked with a smug look gracing his face.

Vlad stood almost to still for a few moments before a smile started to spread across his face. "Charles I couldn't agree with you more. I do have a question, will I be allowed to give my recommendations for his punishment to Andrew and may I witness the the carrying out of his sentence?" Vlad asked. He was now glad that Charles had stopped him from going after Andrew. Vlad could smell the fear rolling off of Ziaran and knew if he did nothing else but remind him everyday that the father of the young vampire that he had killed was going to set in judgment of him.

Charles had already explained everything that was going on and even though Vlad was still upset with Andrew over the sucker punch, he decided that he would let it go. One day he would return the favor but it would end there he even begrudgingly had to admit to himself he was impressed that Andrew had managed to land the punch. Vlad had to wonder to himself if was that he was getting slower or Andrew was just that fast. Vlad laughed inwardly at the thought that he would have to test Andrew once this was over to see if he could land a similar punch again.

"Vlad you know full well I always allow any victims or their relatives to give their input on how they would like to see the perpetrator punished," Charles replied wondering what Vlad was up to. Vlad had witnessed many trials that Charles had hell he was even a witness in a few of them and had seen first hand that the last thing that Charles does before he retires to consider the sentence was allow and one who was a victim or a relative of the victim to testify has to how they would like to see the offender punished.

Charles gave Vlad a sideways glance before realized what he was doing. Charles had to quickly suppress a smile and couldn't help but think, well played my friend. Vlad was already torturing Ziaran everyone here knew that he was a coward and preyed on those that were weaker than him to prove to himself that he was a man. Charles knew that Vlad would take great pleasure in torturing Ziaran by all means he could and Charles almost wished he had the time to watch Vlad at work.

"Vlad I have already sent work to Emma and she will personally meet you at the airport and escort you and your people to my secure facility. Unfortunately I can only house about a dozen of your people in the under ground part since we are still using part of it for our headquarters but I am sure the rest of your people will be comfortable in the above ground areas. Susan ordered. Then softened her tone before continuing, "Anna will be waiting for you at the facility. She said she to tell you she missed her big brother and was looking forward to seeing him again. I told her you were bringing her a special present."

"Thank you Susan. I have to admit it will be good to see her," Vlad said with a small smile.

"You may be cursing me after you get the bill for the card you gave her," Susan teased. She then continued after she noted Vlad's confusion, "She has been going out shopping with Emma and Misha.

Vlad grimaced then he got a large smile as he teased, "That is fine I will just add it to my bill I give to you since it is your daughter's fault."

"That's fine I know how to write disallowed," Susan responded without missing a beat. Her amusement was evident.

"Well as generous as your offer is I must decline," Fredrick replied as he moved slightly in front of Layla.

"Fredrick please reconsider we don't want to upset your father," The leader pleaded.

"I have a counter offer for you Santos. Leave now and take your men with you and I won't mention this to my father. If you refuse then after we kill you I will call my father and tell him how your coven attacked me and my mate. Are you ready to involve the rest of your coven in this you what happened to the last coven that crossed my father. What is your decision?" Fredrick demanded in a cold hard tone. As he spoke he let his baser side come forward.

"Do you realize how much money those two are worth? I tell you what we'll split it with you; all you have to do is walk away. Come on what do you say?" Santos practically begged. He knew that the three of them would have trouble with the blonde they could sense she was an older then the four of them and from her posture it was clear that she wasn't going anywhere.

"Santos do you know who that blonde you are drooling over is? Let me help she is Gloria Vegas number one to Susan Dorchester err now Black as in Charles Black's mate," Fredrick quickly explained.

Santos eyes widened in shock and he visually palled. "Y...You are lying. Why would someone such as her be helping the likes of them," Santos stammered trying to put as much bravado as he could muster.

"For two reason first and most important they are my friends and secondly I owe them my life," Gloria declared as she brought her baser side forward.

"You should have left while you had the chance," Fredrick sadly stated as he started to move towards them

Santos knew unless he came up with a way to prevent it quickly he and his cohorts would be dead. He quickly glanced across the five vampires that now faced them and knew what they had to do. "Get Layla," He mentally screamed the others. Since they were his creations he could mentally speak to them.

Amelia quickly read what Santos was planning and relayed it to Andrew and before any of the others could react to Santos' order, Andrew launched his attack and before Santos knew what was happening Andrew had cleanly removed his head. The two vampires to his left started to charge Layla as they were instructed to, one of them made the mistake of locking eyes with Amelia who promptly took control of him. The other one ran straight into Fredrick who grabbed him by the throat and held him. Fredrick hadn't wanted to kill any of them he would if he had to but he preferred not to kill unless there was no other choice. As he held the young vampire he was less than a year old he wondered why Andrew had attacked all of a sudden.

The final vampire who had Santos' first couldn't believe how quickly his creator had lost his head that quickly and raised his hands in surrender praying that they would be merciful and grant him a quick painless death. Gloria restrained him until they decided what to do with him.

"Andrew why did you suddenly attack them?" Layla asked.

"Amelia read his plan he had ordered the others to get a hold of you and use you as a bargaining chip. Now what are we going to do with them?" Andrew responded.

"Just what the fuck were you all trying to do Miguel?" Fredrick asked.

"We heard that those two were on the roof and we trying to capture them for the reward," Miguel answered quickly pointing at Andrew and Amelia.

"Who told you this?" Fredrick continued his interrogation.

"Javier, one of Mr. Rodrigues' men called. He said that they had some of his men pinned down around here and if we could found the location all we had to do was report it to him and he would pay us handsomely. We heard the gun fire and followed it to here. Santos thought we get the whole reward if we just capture you all ourselves," Miguel replied nervously.

"Did Santos call Javier back and tell them where the shooting was coming from?" Andrew butted in.

"Yes he did about ten minutes ago," the young vampire replied nervously.

Andrew, really didn't want to have to kill the three of them but he knew if they just let them go one or more of them would track their movements and report it to this Javier then they would be in trouble. There was no way the five of them would survive the kind of forces that Rodrigues could and would bring down on them. He glanced at Amelia hoping she would have a suggestion besides wiping their minds.

She smiled, "I know how to handle this." Amelia locked eyes with each one of them taking control of their minds and instructed them to go home and avoid Javier or anyone else associated with Rodrigues. Once they were there, they would sleep for the next two days and when they woke up they would forget all about meeting any of them. She told them if asked to say as far they knew that Santos left town on business and wouldn't be returning anytime soon. She had them repeat their instruction back to her before releasing them.

While Amelia was taking care of the other vampires Andrew called Dafne. She answered on the second ring, "Where are you? What is taking so long?" She asked before Andrew could say anything.

"We got held up there were four young vampires trying to get up on the roof to capture us. One of Rodrigues' men told them it was us on the roof and they were going to try to collect the bounty for themselves. The real bad news is they called Javier before we got here," Andrew quickly explained

"Dammit, OK change of plan I will meet you down there in five minutes. I am going to try to get them to release Augustine then I will be down meanwhile get us transportation," Dafne quickly ordered. She knew that time was now quickly running out and that if they didn't leave in the next ten to fifteen minutes they most likely wouldn't ever leave at least not alive.

Andrew relayed what Dafne had said to the rest of the group. "We will take care of getting us some wheels. Meanwhile you three try to help speed up your guardian angel. If anything happens just ring my cell," Fredrick said as he and Layla took off to get them a vehicle.

Gloria walked over to the door and in less than thirty seconds had managed to pick the lock. Andrew and Amelia quickly followed her through the door making sure to lock it behind them. They knew that the door being locked wouldn't prevent vampires from gaining entrance but it would hopefully provide them a little more time to prepare for an attack all three of them were now hurrying up the stairs as quickly as possible.

Dafne knew that their time was limited if she failed to convince them to leave she would have to call Susan and have to have her rescue Augustine. She hated to have to do it but it was far more important to get the parvulus out of here.

"CP you still there love?" Dafne asked after taking a moment to center herself.

"I am still here, what can I do for you?" Cherry responded.

"I am going to make you a once in a lifetime offer with a thirty second expiration timer. All of you drop your packs, weapons and cell phones and leave now I will allow you to live but if any of you break the deal I will kill each and every one of you. If you agree send Augustine out if not make your peace."

Cherry quickly looked at the others and every one of them were nodding their acceptance while pleading for her to take the deal with their eyes. "We accept the deal but can I please have a couple minutes to feed Raf this blood," Cherry requested.

"You may but first release Augustine and tell him to leave the area. If any of you are try to follow him or stop him I will be watching.

"Dafne this Augustine, I am staying just have them leave I will be safe," Augustine firmly stated.

"Hard headed stupid son-of- bitch. OK Fine just stand by the window to the left where I can see you until they leave," Dafne grumbled before she ordered, "OK, the rest of you drop your packs and weapons, turn out all of your pockets. Lift your pant legs and bottom of your shirts so I can see if you are hiding anything."

"Miss, May I keep my wallet it only has pictures of my family in it," one of the younger ones asked.

"You may just hold it in your hands and that goes for the rest of you take your wallets and if you have any money you can take it also. Raf I am sure Susan will be billing you for the blood and all of the damages to her building I would suggest you pay the bill and not make me come collect it from you," Dafne harshly stated. She watched as Cherry disarmed Rafael showing her that he was indeed disarmed she held up his wallet and money then stuck them in his shirt pocket.

"Dafne I know you said to hold that shit in our hands but he is going to have to be carried out," Cherry said.

"No problem get one of the others to help you carry him out of there. They can place their wallets in there shirt pocket also. Now get moving before I change my mind," Dafne ordered.

The mercenaries didn't need to be told a second time they quickly exited the building and loaded up in their four Expeditions and took off as if the devil himself was chasing them. Dafne watched them until they got a few miles away then breathed a sigh of relief until she sensed someone moving up behind her. She quickly spun and covered the door that led to the roof. She tensed as the door opened slightly

"Dafne! It's Andrew, please hold your fire," Andrew announced loudly.

"OK, come on out," Dafne said keeping her rifle ready just encase. Once she saw it was Andrew, Amelia and to her surprise Gloria she lowered the rifle, "what the hell I thought I told you to arrange for transportation for us and wait for me in the alley."

"Fredrick and Layla are handling the transportation issues, so we came up to see if we can be have help," Andrew explained keeping his tone calm.

"Very well please let Augustine know you are safe and convince that idiot to close up the store for today Rodrigues isn't going to be happy you all got away and may decide to take out on him," Dafne quickly explained

Gloria quickly grabbed the cell that was still on speaker and switched it to normal. "Augustine, it is Gloria we are all safe I want you to get the hell out of there now...I don't care and neither will Susan... Meet your employees by where the tunnel exit is and all of you get out of town for a few days I will call Susan and have her handle the facility... go to the safe house near Morelia Susan will contact you there." Gloria ordered then softened her voice, "Augustine please be careful, I don't want to lose any more friends."

Gloria quickly disconnected the call, she would contact Susan once they were on the road she followed the rest of them down the eight flights of stairs. All of them were almost running down the stairs racing to make a clean getaway. However as they exited the building they saw three black Escalades setting there and everyone froze as they looked at the nine very large, heavily armed vampires standing their waiting on them. Not a one of them had sensed them. Andrew and Dafne who were in the lead immediate let their baser side come forward.

"Dafne, Andrew, Charles sent us. We are to escort you to meet him. We must hurry Rodrigues' men are about ten minutes out." The one who was the leader quickly explained as he handed a letter to Andrew.

"They work for Charles," Gloria quickly informed the others after she saw who they were.

Andrew was just about to attack when he heard Gloria's announcement. He quickly reigned in his baser side it was then then he noticed Layla and Fredrick standing beside two of the men and not under any duress.

"I am sorry to rush you but we must make haste," The leader quickly urged everyone. All six of them were quickly ushered into the middle Expedition along with the leader and what Andrew assumed was the second in command buy the way he acted.

"I must apologize for my manners I am William Lentz but please call me bill and this is my eldest son Eli," Bill introduced himself after they were one their way.

"Where are we meeting Charles?" Amelia asked she was still little wary of them. She could sense that Andrew was also but with him unless you could read his mind you never know it.

"We are meeting him near Oaxaca. Not to worry you all are in good hands," Bill said with a reassuring smile.

Amelia took a quick peek at his mind and found his mind closed off to her. She mentally said to Andrew, "Love, I cannot pierce his mental shield." as she replied aloud with a painted smile, "Thank you for the lift,"

Amelia quickly peak into Eli's mind and found that they were indeed working for Charles and had been assigned to protect them until they could meet up with

Charles and Susan. She quickly relayed her finding to Andrew allowing both of them to finally relax.

"About how long will it take us?" Andrew asked suddenly feeling a little worn no that the adrenaline was leaving his system. .

"About five hours. Andrew are you feeling OK?" Gloria asked. She noticed how peaked Andrew looked. She wondered when he had last fed but recalled he had drank some blood while they were at Susan's facility.

"I'm fine just feeling a little fatigued. I everything is finally catching up to me," Andrew replied. He knew he was not feeling right but he figured it was just a combination of him running at full steam for the last few weeks and the additional stress of him fighting with his baser side for control after what happened to Jake.

Amelia snuggled up beside her mate she was also concerned about how Andrew looked and was praying he was right. She had taken a quick peak into his mind to make sure that he really as calm as he seemed and for now he was on an even keel more at peace with himself then he had been since Jake was taken. She could still sense his anger and sorrow but he was a lot calmer then she had expected him to be.

Amelia heard Andrew breathing soften as he drifted off to sleep and it lured her into a restful sleep. Gloria looked over at her two friends was glad to see that they had finally drifted off to sleep. She suddenly remembered she needed to call Susan to update her and also let her know that she had sent Augustine and the other employees to the safe house near Morelia. Susan was just updating her on the capture of Ziaran when Amelia and Andrew suddenly bolted up almost standing up in the truck. Gloria saw that Amelia's eyes were glowing.

"Tell Susan that Charles and her need to get the fuck out of there now. They are about to be attacked and if they stay they will die," Amelia frantically warned.

"She is right I saw it also," Andrew quickly added his voice to hers

Gloria didn't need to repeat Amelia's words to Susan she heard them and was quickly relaying them to Charles when his cell started to ring. She heard Emma say, "Dad you and mom need to leave where ever you are now Catherine is frantic saying if you don't leave right now you're going to die. Please listen to her."

"Don't worry sweetie we're leaving immediately. I'll call you back as soon as we are airborne," Charles reassured Emma.

"Gloria tell Amelia we are leaving. I will call you once we're airborne to arrange a new meet point," Susan quickly said.

"Bridgette tell Swede I want to be airborne ASAP," Charles ordered.

Everyone boarded as the crew quickly went through their preflight checks and started the engines at the same time knowing this was far from the proper procedures but knowing that their lives depended on them getting done as quickly as possible. In less than fifteen minutes the plane was taxing down the runway gaining speed to leap into the air. He had purchased the farm and made the hidden runway over years ago. When he first made the runway it was only capable of handling a small commuter plane he had lengthen it to be able to handle the largest airliners made today. He had a large hanger disguised as a barn to hide the planes which is equipped with all of the tools and equipment needed to properly service and maintain the aircraft. The runway had been camouflaged to look as if it was part or wheat field.

Charles watched as vehicles speed down his long driveway loaded with men and he sighed knowing that his and Susan retreat was now gone. The two of them would secret away here to renew their spirits and get away from everyone. He always loved their time here it had strengthened their bond even though they weren't mated. He had went to great lengths to make sure that only a few knew the location of this hideaway and now it was ruined. Perhaps the most troubling part was that if Amsu had managed to locate this place meant that one of his most trusted friends had betrayed him and that along with the betrayal of the man he had come to think of as his father made Charles feel old and worn out.

Susan sensing the change in Charles mood walked over to him and plopped down in his lap laying her head against his chest. Instinctively Charles wrapped his arm around her soaking in the warmth and comfort she was providing. "We will get through this and be stronger for it. Our new family will help to make that happen," Susan softly whispered.

"Charles where are we heading to now?" Swede asked over the intercom.

"Head to TLJ." Charles responded after a couple moments.

"Charles I'm not sure that is a good idea we really need to get back to friendlier ground. I understand you want to help Andrew and Amelia but we can't afford to lose you. Not to mention since they are mobile and traveling with Bill's group they shouldn't have any trouble meeting us at the California border," Kirk argued.

Charles went to object but Kirk cut him off, Charles it will be safer for them also I know how important they're to you and Susan but we aren't exactly in an inconspicuous vehicle here and with limited options were we can land it all Amsu has to do is check to see which airport we are heading to it will have to be one of the larger ones unless you have another piece of property down here I know nothing about," Kirk finished his argument.

Charles sighed deeply his shoulders slumped slightly, "I guess you are right. Susan please call Bill on the secure SAT. Phone," Charles conceded unwillingly.

Susan dialed the number but Charles quickly refocused himself and asked for the phone he knew it was his responsibility to tell them they had to try to make it on their own. "Bill it is Charles. Please put me on speaker," Charles said once the phone was answered.

Bill quickly did as requested he had a sinking feeling about this call. "OK, boss the phone is on speaker."

"Everyone I hate to have to inform you that you all are going to have to try to get back to California on your own. I will try to help you as much as possible but the general concern here is if try to land the jet anywhere in Mexico Rodrigues and Amsu will be able to get people in place to intercept us long before we land," Charles sadly stated his voice filled with regret.

"Charles we understand and know if there were any way possible for you pick us up you do it but I have to agree with the others it would be too dangerous. We will see you and Susan soon," Amelia replied before anyone else could but the others quickly added their voices to her.

"Andrew just to let you know the man who had Jake killed is now in our custody. I can promise you he is as uncomfortable as he possible can be made Vlad is seeing to that personally. I have decided that once he is done testifying to other enforcers you will set in judgment of him. You will have final say in what is to happen to him but I will ask one favor please at least consider Vlad's recommendation he and his family has suffered a lot because of Ziaran," Charles said.

"Thank you Charles and I will be glad for any suggestions Vlad or anyone else has," Andrew replied. They talked for a few more minutes before they ended the call agreeing that they would contact Charles once they were across the border.

Charles hung up the phone with a heavy heart he wanted to go pick them up but had reluctantly agreed all he would accomplish was getting all of them captured or killed. He silent stared out the window wondering if would ever see his friends again.

"OK, how do we go from here?" Andrew asked looking at Bill.

Bill punched up a map of the US/Mexican border and began to study it. He was looking for an area where they could cross with relative ease. The trouble was it would be a breeze for them to get through customs once they made it to the border however since Rodrigues controlled a large portion of the police and military he could easily use them to make sure they would never make it to the border.

Fredrick was looking at the same map that Bill was and came to the same conclusion that bill did. He set their trying to come up with a plan that would greatly increase their chances of survival. Fredrick had one advantage over bill his father's organization was spread throughout Mexico and the northern part of South America.

"Bill I have an idea. Head for the Universidad Mesoamericana Del Centro in Puebla. I know of a place near there that we can get a little rest, food, blood and most important of all a different set of wheels," Fredrick suggested.

Bill looked at the others in the car and they all nodded seeming to agree with Fredrick. He then considered the alternatives and saw few he knew by now Rodrigues would have all of the crossing covered. He called the other two vehicles and told them to follow him. As they were driving all attention was turned to Fredrick.

"My plan is that we let the rest of your men take the three Expeditions and head towards Brownsville Texas as long as we aren't with them they should be able to get through any road blocks and if they are questioned by one of Rodrigues' men they can say that they are heading home. I do believe that Amelia would be able to implant a couple of memories that will keep them safe. She should be able to place a temporary block in their mind that will clear once they see Charles or Susan.

Either way we mustn't let them know where we are going for everyone safety. We won't be heading north but south. I will contact my father and have him spread the word that we are heading towards Cancun basically let Rodrigues believe we are going after him. We however will be heading towards Guatemala La Aurora International Airport. I choose this course for two reasons one it will be out of Rodrigues' territory and secondly I have a friend here that can get us all of the paper work we need to get to California." Fredrick explained.

"OK let's say I agree to this plan in principle but I have a couple of questions. First of all, why not take my men with us? Secondly, how long do you think it will take us to get there and acquire the paperwork we need to get back to the states and can you really trust this person of yours not to turn us in for the reward?" Bill asked. He really didn't care for making his men act as a decoy they were friends and sons or daughters of friends. Lastly he was unsure of the young man that was standing before him he could see that the others trusted him but he knew of his father. He knew that Peppy was generally known to be a man of his word however Bill knew that Peppy in addition to his legal businesses ran a large criminal organization that was known to break not only human laws but also vampire ones including human trafficking. Fredrick was supposed to be being groomed to replace his father and as such he handle all of his father's organizations problems. If rumors are to be believed with remarkable efficiency.

"I do not think my mother's oldest brother would betray me and my parents, do you?" Fredrick snapped back.

Bill quickly raised his hands in surrender gesture, "I meant no disrespect I am only trying to keep you all and especially my son safe."

"I apologize, I shouldn't have snapped at you like that," Fredrick said with regret.

"Bill perhaps it would be better if you and your son went with your men we will be fine," Gloria suggested.

"Gloria, you of all people know I can't and won't do that Charles order me to keep you all safe and I refuse to disobey him no matter what the cost," Bill replied hesitantly.

"Bill, Gloria is correct it would better for all of us if we split up. We all appreciate all of the help you and your men have been. As far as Charles I will make sure he knows it was our decision," Andrew stated hoping to end the debate.

"Andrew it isn't going to happen. My orders are to keep you safe and I intend to follow those orders no matter how I have to do it. I intend to follow my orders with or without your cooperation," Bill ordered sternly.

"Bill, I would suggest you change your tone. You aren't in charge of us. I should also warn you that Neither Amelia nor Andrew take threats well," Gloria warned.

"I am sorry I didn't intend that to sound like a threat. I was just trying to make you all understand that the game has changed dramatically and I'm very uncomfortable using my people as decoys it is a sure way to get them tortured and killed if Rodrigues' men capture them even if Amelia is capable of doing what you say. You have to understand they are like family to me," Bill apologies.

"Bill, I understand but if we have three Expeditions traveling in a convoy we will draw attention we need to split up. This will give your men their best chance to survive," Amelia suggested.

Bill turned slightly in his seat so he could face Amelia as he spoke to her. As he looked past her to the road behind them he seemed to zone out for a moment his eyes fixed on something behind them. "Shit!" he cursed quietly, so quietly that if everyone would have been human, they would of never heard it. He then pointed as he announced, "It may be too late."

THE END